Life's a Cocktail

Life's a Cocktail

Richenda van Laun

Life's a Cocktail
Richenda van Laun

Published by Aspect Design 2017
Malvern, Worcestershire, United Kingdom.

Designed, printed and bound by Aspect Design
89 Newtown Road, Malvern, Worcs. WR14 1PD
United Kingdom
Tel: 01684 561567
E-mail: allan@aspect-design.net
Website: www.aspect-design.net

ISBN 978-1-912078-63-9

To those of my family and friends
whose uplifting support and love is always there.

Life's a Cocktail

In the corner of a school playground, partially hidden by a tree, a frightened girl was being bullied and verbally abused.

Ever since her arrival at St Anselm's School, Sophia had been picked on by two, sometimes three girls. Today, after being lured there with the promise of a leaving present, she found herself pinned up against the railings, a gang of five forming a semi-circle round her. Those at either end, having been recruited on the school bus and bribed with a Mars bar or ciggy, had been instructed to give a certain girl 'a mouthful' during break time.

'Feeble, feeble,' they choroused. 'Soppy date, daddy's little girl, or is it grandpa's? So we're leaving school today are we? Good riddance.'

There was no escape and Sophia could only try her best to fend off some of the kicks and punches. Suddenly, one of them pulled a pen knife from her sock and flicked it open. Sophia saw the blade glint in the sun. She screamed.

A pupil walking nearby, hearing a cry of distress, peered round the tree and shouted, 'Pack it in you lot.'

At that moment, the bell rang and Sophia was able to run to the safety of her classroom. Though thoroughly shaken, knowing there could never be a repeat of what happened that morning helped her recover. How thankful she was to be leaving the school.

Later on, Sophia had arranged to meet her two best friends, Holly and Margaret, in the cloakroom. They would often huddle together there, sitting on low wooden benches amid a scattering of smelly gym shoes, to talk about boys and how much they hated the school. Sophia always looked forward to seeing her friends, and particularly today when they would exchange small presents and arrange to meet in the hols to see a flick. She prayed that they wouldn't notice the red marks on her arms and legs.

During the last four years she had been picked on by the same three girls, who used foul language and attempted to kick and punch her, and until now she had been able to hide the odd bruise.

Holly and Margaret were ready and waiting, but when Sophia appeared they noticed the marks on her legs and pale face.

'Sofe, you look awful, what's up?' asked Holly.

Feelings of shame had always stopped her from revealing anything about being bullied, but it now seemed impossible to keep it to herself any longer.

'I think I must be a really horrible person.'

'What on earth do you mean?' cried Margaret.

With huge relief Sophia poured out her dreadful experiences over the last four years. She was especially hurt by the suggestion from one of this morning's attackers that her father was really her grandfather.

Having listened with concern, Margaret put an arm round her.

'I'll tell you what it's about,' she said, 'they're eaten up with jealousy because you've got the best figure in the school and fantastic copper-coloured hair *and* you're a very special person.'

She was grateful for such warmth and understanding as earlier that afternoon, when told to see the headmistress, she was met with the coldness of a fish. Miss Carter's opening remark was no surprise.

'You are making a great mistake by not staying to take School

Certificate. We all know you don't like it here and you have made little effort to contribute anything to St Anselm's. You'll never do any good. Please send the next girl in.'

The headmistress's final remark did not bother her at all as she knew it to be completely untrue.

Outside a nervous threesome had waited, all of whom had taken part in the morning's bullying. Seeing Sophia two of them scowled and the other looked tearful.

'Next one,' said Sophia giving them an icy look.

Leaving the dingy cloakroom the three made their way up some steps and into the sunshine. As she did so Sophia's sense of freedom was as a snake shedding its skin. With a final wave she walked through the school gates to where her father would be waiting in the car to take her home.

As they drove off he asked how she had acquired the bruise on her leg and graze on her cheek.

'I fell in the playground. It's nothing.'

'Oh, bad luck.' Knowing his daughter, he asked no further questions.

Once they were well out of sight of the school, however, Sophia began to talk with excitement about all the possibilities which might lie ahead. A different girl now sat beside him and whatever path she decided to tread, he would back her every step of the way.

For the past year, Sophia had pleaded that on reaching the age of sixteen she be allowed to leave school, regularly making the point that because she was miserable at St A's—as it was known—failing her exams was almost a certainty. Her exhausted parents finally gave in.

A similar situation had arisen when a seven-year-old Sophia

had told her parents firmly that, needing the companionship of other girls, she wished to go away to boarding school. With help towards fees from a family member, a year later Sophia found herself at Hindyford and it suited her perfectly. Lessons were enjoyable and her talent in the wonderful art room was quickly spotted and encouraged, as was her ability in the saddle, as a competent and quite competitive rider. Her weekly letter home was full of enthusiasm and never failed to say how happy she was. It was little wonder therefore that St A's seemed more like a prison with its dreary uniform and long list of absurd rules. Soon after arriving it was as though a part of her had closed down. Any subject, or anything at which she showed promise, seemed to be ignored or crushed. At Hindyford she had been somebody, here she was nobody.

Sitting together that evening, Sophia's parents saw a sparkle in her eye and became aware that her optimistic nature—which had been missing for so long—was re-emerging, and realised that despite their misgivings, Sophia had again made the right choice.

Pat Shaw considered herself a rather elderly parent. Finding she was pregnant at forty-two was rather a shock. Once past the morning sickness stage, however, she saw it as a welcome surprise. Their son, Daniel, had arrived fourteen years ago and she and Rupert were perfectly happy with an only child.

Having suffered quite severe wounds during the First World War, Rupert had become rather withdrawn and never spoke of his experiences. He had always been a kind and faithful husband, and while not being the most exciting companion, was unfailingly helpful and considerate. Privately, he had rather dreaded the thought of a bawling baby in the house, but as it turned out, Sophia, who was born just before the outbreak of the

Second World War, was a content little girl, and quickly became the apple of his eye.

Pat and Rupert, anticipating their daughter's likely plan for the immediate future of being a waitress in a coffee bar, had made sure of securing a place with a local tutor, where she would have a year to pass School Certificate. Much to their surprise and relief, the arrangement was been happily accepted.

Sophia realised immediately that they had settled on the perfect compromise. She liked the idea of a small group in a setup which, she hoped, would allow the independence she craved. As a loving daughter, she guessed how much effort had been put into making the arrangements for her final year of education and silently vowed to put all the energy she could muster into getting good exam results.

A year later, Sophia left the tutor, having achieved very good marks in art and passes in English and geography. She had been happy there and found the group of boys and girls pleasant enough without wishing to make any particular friends. Her whole aim had been to pass School Certificate and she found, a little unexpectedly, she had been able to apply herself and stick rigidly to her plan.

When the results arrived in the midday post, Sophia detected a look of disappointment on her mother's face.

'Look,' she said, 'I did my best and I'm afraid you'll have to accept I'm not academic.'

'I think you did jolly well,' her father said, handing her a celebratory glass of sherry before their lunch.

'Thanks, Pop, and you know you and Mum need never worry about me, 'cos I'll always be alright.'

Pat, praying that none of their friends would ask about Sophia's results, added, 'We know you're a very capable girl and, by the way, we're so looking forward to this special meal you've prepared.'

Sophia had indeed spent several hours the previous day

making Coronation chicken and trifle. It had been a real labour of love and she was proud of herself.

'It's all ready and I'm starving.'

Sophia led the way into the dining room, and as they settled themselves at the table, she glanced from one parent to the other.

'I'd love to know what you've got planned for me next.' She knew, at just seventeen, her parents would have chatted to their friends about what to do with her. After flirting with the idea of waitressing, her only aspirations had been a petrol pump attendant or a cowgirl on a ranch in America. Both quite out of the question, of course, as any adult member of the family would undoubtedly say.

Seeing anxious looks exchanged, Sophia braced herself for the answer.

'Well, darling, we think shorthand and typing would be so useful—always something to fall back on.'

A grey cloud descended on Sophia. She simply couldn't see herself as an efficient secretary in a smart little suit.

'Oh, alright, I suppose so.'

A lack of interest had been anticipated so, looking brighter, Pat continued, 'There's a treat in store, however. You and your cousin Ruth have been invited to stay in London with Granny to do the Season.'

'Don't know much about it, only that in the old days girls hoped to pick up a husband, their mum's idea being to get them off their hands.'

This was not the reaction Pat had hoped for, but she continued, 'Of course, young ladies have to earn a living nowadays, it's just a wonderful opportunity to have great fun for a short time.'

Pat had conveniently forgotten that, when she did the Season, thinking herself not as pretty as many of the other girls, she had constantly feared rejection. Sophia, therefore, only heard about the way she was waltzed off her feet at glamorous balls.

Knowing the look on her mother's face, the same old story was about to be repeated.

Fortunately, lunch was finished and Sophia was able to excuse herself. 'Sorry, Mum, I've got some washing up to do.'

Before starting the shorthand and typing course, Sophia put her time to good use. Always aware that her parents were older than those of her friends, she painted and decorated, did a little weeding and found she was a natural and enthusiastic cook. Now, as her parents—particularly her father—were showing signs of ageing, she was more than capable of helping them in practical ways and would undertake almost any job. As long as riding still featured in her life, she was happy.

Horses were in her blood and until she was fourteen, when boys started to take over, she had owned a pony and learned that the price you paid for equine ownership was the discipline of looking after your four-legged friend. Wisely, her parents seldom offered to help, leaving her to cope with wind, rain and mud on a winter's evening.

Nowadays, she depended on friends for rides. One of them had quarter horses and Sophia found Western riding fascinating, particularly the 'moves' the animals were trained to do, each having a practical application for rounding up cattle.

All too soon the future had to be faced and it was time to start the shorthand and typing course in London.

From the first day, Sophia found it hard-going and boring. Her brain didn't seem to function in the right way. She resented having to do the course, but was rather looking forward to doing the Season after all.

The highlight of the day was the lunch break when a small

group of them would go to Lyons Corner House for a bite to eat. She would then scour the shops in and around Oxford Street for evening dresses. Her grandmother would regard the area as 'rather common', but Sophia, with the small allowance her parents could manage, was clever at finding inexpensive clothes and adapting them. She was skilled with a needle and could create something with style from a very ordinary dress. To enhance the new wardrobe, she found some pretty pieces of jewellery in the Portobello Road Market.

On the final day of the course, the college informed Sophia that, with luck, she might hold down a job which did not require great speed on the typewriter. It was no surprise, but disappointing nevertheless.

When she and her group went for a final cup of tea at Lyons Corner House, she discovered most of the other girls had done well and poor Sophia felt rather a failure.

It was fortunate that she and her cousin Ruth were moving into their grandmother's flat that evening. Ruth always made her laugh which lifted her spirits. She could forget the course and look forward to the start of the Season.

Having settled themselves in, the two girls sat on Ruth's bed to chat. Sophia's cousin was better informed and had a good idea of what lay ahead.

'Come on, Ruth, tell me all about it!'

'Well, it starts with mothers' lunches and they talk about dates for dances and exchange lists of suitable men. Some have NSIT by their names.'

'What on earth does that mean?' asked Sophia.

'Not safe in taxis!'

'Could be fun,' laughed Sophia.

Spot on 8.55 pm, Granny appeared at the door.

'Come and listen to the news and then it'll be bedtime for chicks.'

The girls pulled faces, but knew they were expected to be

on best behaviour at all times. The last thing they wanted to do was listen to the boring old news.

Sophia did not feel comfortable with her grandmother and if it had not been for Ruth's presence, she would certainly have not stayed on her own. The flat rather reflected her grandmother's personality, not cosy like her own home, but austere and cold. The hall was long with dark portraits of severe-looking people and the drawing room an arrangement of hard chairs and unforgiving chaises longues. She was, Sophia had to admit, extremely generous as she would provide for all their domestic needs for several months.

The following afternoon, the girls, who were enjoying looking at their shoes and dresses, were disturbed by the door bell.

'I think that'll be Mum.' Sophia opened the door to a rather breathless Pat. 'Welcome to Gloom Hall, Mum.'

'Shhh, darling.'

'It's alright, Granny's gone to the Army and Navy Stores. Come in and sit down. Ruth's here and we'll make some tea.'

Having selected the least hard chair, Pat slowly lowered herself down and drew in her breath.

'I've got some wonderful news . . . Granny's going to give a dance for you and Ruth.'

Sophia was, more than anything, relieved by this announcement. She had been concerned that her parents would try to find the money, perhaps by selling some of the family furniture in order to pay for a dance. Free of this worry, she allowed herself to look forward to it knowing that quite a number of invitations would be received and that hospitality could be returned.

After enjoying two welcome cups of tea, Pat continued, 'This is a most generous and kind offer and we must all show our gratitude when she returns from shopping. Here's a plant to give Granny,' she said reaching into one of her many shopping bags, 'and we'll treat her to a nice lunch very soon.'

In no time invitations started to arrive for Ruth and Sophia. Firstly for tea parties, followed by cocktail parties and dances. Sophia was soon running a finger over the cards—embossed? Mmmm, or not.

Before long, she was off to her first tea party. As instructed by Ruth, the most important item in her handbag was not a lipstick, but an address book.

Nervously pressing the doorbell, she found herself ushered into a roomful of girls. Thankfully, she spotted two familiar faces from near home, one being her friend Holly. They had been unable to meet since school, so had a great deal to talk about. After sandwiches and delicious chocolate cake, they all circulated, address books at the ready. You must come to my dance was the cry. Sophia thoroughly enjoyed herself and most especially meeting a girl who introduced herself as Georgina. She was friendly, warm and fun, and keen that they should meet for lunch soon.

A highlight of the Season were the Presentations. Sophia was no exception in finding the idea of curtsying to the Queen quite daunting. A well-meaning relation had given her a cast-off dress in which to go, but when Sophia tried it on she instantly hated it. As her clothes allowance would not stretch to buying a new afternoon frock, she had to simply grin and bear it. Pat therefore had no inkling of her daughter's feelings and was able to anticipate with pleasure another visit to the palace. It had been a wonderful occasion for her and she was sure it would be for Sophia too. Even Pop, usually reluctant to leave his garden, was showing enthusiasm. As a soldier, the mention of 'if in possession, swords should be worn' on the invitation seemed to please him.

Before being presented, however, Sophia found she was expected to have lessons on how to curtsy. At the final session, having mastered the technique, she felt a tap on her shoulder. A tall, dark girl whom she hadn't yet spoken to whispered, 'The Duke of Edinburgh might wink when you curtsy to him. Did you know that?'

This information made Sophia visualise herself wobbling perilously. Seeing her look of concern, the girl introduced herself.

'My name's Caroline and don't worry, just avoid eye contact with him, and the Queen.'

'Thanks for telling me. I'm Sophia Shaw. Is there anything else I need to know?'

'Tell you what, come back to my house when we've finished here 'cos my sister was presented two years ago. She'll be very helpful.'

Caroline's elder sister was able to pass on some useful tips, and made Sophia laugh about the Queen having to look over the curtsying girls heads as she had found the continuous bobbing up and down made her feel seasick.

A plan was made to meet again before the Presentations; conveniently they lived only a couple of bus stops from each other. Sophia felt she had met someone who, while being good company, seemed straight forward, dependable and altogether delightful.

On the afternoon of the Presentations, Sophia was too agitated to enjoy or appreciate the occasion. There seemed to be endless waiting and sitting on little gold chairs, but she at least managed the curtsies without mishap. After an exhausting afternoon, it was a relief to get back to the flat, fling the awful dress on the floor, put on her jeans and unwind with a cup of tea. It was many years later that she realised how privileged she had been, especially as they came to an end the following year.

A whirlwind of parties was now well underway. Much to Sophia's relief, rather than arriving on your own at a dance, dinner parties for around a dozen were given by the parents of an invited deb. You would then get to the dance at 10 pm as part of a group. Sophia, once on the dance floor, became very animated and many of the young men found her attractive. For her part, having been told that her dancing partners would be smooth debs' delights or chinless wonders, which some were, she found most of them intelligent, kind and amusing. A few who were always in demand for dances could depend on getting fed for a whole Season. They certainly got dinner, and often breakfast at the end of a dance.

Another big occasion was Queen Charlotte's Ball when all the girls wore white dresses. Beforehand, Sophia met her friends Georgina and Caroline; the latter was keen on history and wanted to tell them how the ball came about. Sophia knew that Queen Charlotte was the wife of George III and had produced lots of children, so looked forward to hearing more.

Every year, Caroline told them, Queen Charlotte had celebrated her birthday with family and maids of honour who brought the cake in, which she then cut herself. She was a compassionate person and took a special interest in poor women who were ill in childbirth or homeless. The first hospital for women, Queen Charlotte's Hospital, was named after her. Caroline explained that each year a number of debs were specially chosen to bring in the cake, now only cardboard!

At the insistence of her mother, Sophia had a dress made for the occasion which, despite several fittings, did not look or feel right. It did nothing for her confidence and the evening was a disaster. Another on the list, albeit short, of 'hated it'. Sophia felt rather indifferent about some of the dances, but would click with at least one dancing partner and all would be well. After each one, she wrote comments on the back of the invitation card. Many years later they would provide much amusement. 'Met Jack—v. nice—he's got an XK150 Jag—heaven' always made her chuckle.

During the flurry of parties and meeting new people, Sophia could claim two boyfriends. Nigel, whom she had met at her shared dance with Ruth as a last minute guest, was solid and dependable and very much in love with her, and Andrew, a dark and handsome Army officer. He seemed the epitome of glamour and she was obsessed with him. One of her many cousins had married at eighteen and Sophia so hoped the same might happen to her. She would often daydream about living in a lovely house with a large dining room in which she could feed and entertain at least ten people.

As the Season wound down she and Andrew would go out, usually to dinner, at least once a week. Sophia had lost her heart completely and her virginity too. But before long, putting it down to Army commitments, she was aware of fewer telephone calls and dates. One day he rang her with an invitation to lunch. It had been longer than usual since hearing from him so it was an exciting surprise.

During the morning of her date with Andrew she made the most of her appearance. Feeling a little nervous, she decided that treating herself to a taxi would help her to arrive in a calm state.

Andrew, already at the restaurant, led her to a small intimate table for two. They had barely started eating when he told Sophia that he was ending their relationship. In seconds her hopes and dreams for the future were shattered and the meal could not be over quickly enough. She could, by then, only manage a brief thank you when she got up to leave. As she did so, Andrew handed her a small box.

The bus home was about to move off as Sophia scrambled on and found a seat. With a beating heart she opened the present and found the box contained a powder compact. Nothing about it appealed to her and even the hinge soon became loose. Had it been pure gold it would of meant nothing, only broken dreams. The rejection was a bolt out the blue, and left her shocked and bewildered. She felt somehow ashamed, and apart from desperately needing to confide in her brother, Daniel, told nobody.

It seemed that quite suddenly there was no more invitations and no more fun and Sophia was deposited back to earth with a nasty bump. Real life had to be faced such as getting a job and finding a flat to share. Despite her sadness, she was aware of being more poised and self-confident and that, after a mere six months, the final step into adulthood had been taken

Ruth, whom Sophia saw less of now, had already found a flat and a good job. It was not long, however, before she heard of two girls needing a third to share accommodation, and after two interviews she secured a position in a travel agents.

As the weeks went by, family and friends were concerned as she looked thin and gaunt, but would reveal little, simply that she was not on top form.

She applied herself as best she could to her job, but was not happy in the flat. The other two girls were old friends and Sophia felt left out.

London was losing its appeal and a plan was starting to form in Sophia's mind. Even the faithful Nigel, having on more than one occasion seen her on Andrew's arm, had taken up with another girl. Meeting friends for the cinema cheered her up, as did going home most weekends. Her parents were 'getting on a bit' as she put it, so she continued to help as much as possible. She tidied the garden reluctantly, but got great satisfaction from painting and decorating. It was good to feel part of a group of local friends again and do some riding. Galloping over the fields put a grin on her face and gave her a greatly improved appetite.

Finally, one weekend, Sophia, looking happier than she had for weeks, told her parents, 'Mum and Pop, I've decided to leave London, rent a little cottage near you and become self-employed'.

Pat looked concerned, 'Oh darling, are you certain this is the right thing? You've been in the job no time.'

'Blow that. I've completely gone off the travel agents and the flat, but managed to save some more money for a van and I plan to work as a painter and decorator.'

Her mother, having already passed on her own small car to Sophia, did not think a van was at all the thing.

Both parents had mixed feelings, especially about the work she proposed to do, but knew better than to try and persuade her otherwise.

Sophia had decided not to tell them about a number of disturbing incidents that had happened in London. It was something she had considered reporting to the police, but lack of information prevented her from doing so.

Not long after starting her job, Sophia noticed a black car following closely on the route to work and sometimes going home. On two or three occasions, it was waiting at the top of her road. The driver, dressed in what looked like a black cloak, with a high collar, large black hat and dark glasses, was impossible to identify as male or female. Sophia became increasingly frightened and nervous of being alone in the flat. Who would want to scare or hurt her? She simply couldn't imagine. Having made lists of everyone she knew, not one of them had a motive for such threatening behaviour.

Apart from her brother, anyone she told might think it entirely made up. She must talk to him. Alone one evening in the flat, Sophia dialled Daniel's number. His wife, Belinda, answered.

'Hold on, Sophia, he's just come in—Your sister. In a bit of a state I think,' she whispered, putting her hand over the mouthpiece.

'Sophia, love, what can I do for you?'

'Have me for the weekend, I hope.'

'Of course. You sound agitated.'

'I am. See you at about six o'clock on Friday. I'll tell you everything then.'

Having made the plan she immediately felt better. Hearing her brother's voice gave her courage.

When Sophia arrived for the weekend, she found doting parents playing with their four-month-old daughter, Serena, and felt her presence was a little intrusive.

However, once the baby was in bed, they were able to relax

with a drink. Daniel was keen to hear all about this 'coming out caper', so Sophia did her best to entertain them with stories of the wonderful dances she'd been to and all the new and interesting people she had met. He had already heard a little about her love life and enquired, 'By the way, how's Andrew?'

The look she gave him said it all. Later in the kitchen, over the washing up, he said, 'I can see you're bursting to tell me. We'll be on our own at breakfast.'

'Thanks, Daniel. You're right, I can't wait to talk to you,' a relieved Sophia answered.

That night, as her head hit the pillow, she enjoyed the first peaceful night's sleep in quite a while.

The following morning, over coffee and toast, she told Daniel how very hurt she was by Andrew's rejection.

'My dear sister, I think you're well rid of him,' Daniel reassured her firmly. 'He's arrogant and spoilt and you're worth more.'

'You've made me feel miles better, so no more tears. I need to talk to you about something else though . . . I'm being followed.'

'Meaning?'

'Driving to and from work, there's nearly always a black car behind me. The driver is wearing a big black hat and dark glasses so it's impossible to see if it's a man or a woman. Twice they've been waiting at the top of my road.'

'Get the registration number for a start,' suggested Daniel.

'How can I when I'm driving?'

'Okay, well, you could try changing your route to and from work.'

'I'll do that . . . what really worries me is that it must be someone I know. I'm so scared, Daniel. I don't like being on my own in the flat. I can only talk to you—anyone else would think I was mad.'

Daniel put a comforting arm round his rather pale sister.

'I've got to go to America for two weeks, but in the meantime could you talk to Ruth? She's completely down to earth and sensible.'

Sophia shook her head. 'No, she's busy getting engaged and can't think of anything else. What could anybody do anyway? No one has physically hurt me, so the police can't help.'

'What about your new friends, Caroline or Georgina? You need to at least get it off your chest to someone.'

'Maybe . . . by the way, please don't mention anything to Mum and Pop. I don't want to worry them.'

The following week, as Daniel suggested, Sophia took a different route to work, without incident. Her brother was right—just someone playing a silly prank. For the next few days, Sophia was confident she had shaken off her stalker, until one evening there was the black car waiting near the flat. Her blood ran cold, and as she passed Sophia looked through the window and screamed with fear, for the driver was wearing the most terrifying mask.

She stumbled into the flat and went straight to the telephone. Thankfully, Daniel answered immediately, but she was already sobbing hysterically.

'Calm down, Sophia, love. Tell me what's happened.'

'I can't stay in London,' was all she could manage.

It was a few minutes before she could speak, but she was then able to describe the masked figure and how it had made her feel sick with fear. 'I thought everything was back to normal and now this happens.'

'Tell you what,' said Daniel, 'we're coming up for the theatre tonight. We'll collect you afterwards—about 10.30, so start packing.'

'Daniel—nobody could ask for a more fantastic brother. You're a life saver. Thank you so much.'

Sophia immediately began throwing clothes and possessions into suitcases, remembering to leave a note and money for rent.

With time to kill before Daniel's arrival, she tidied her bedroom and then forced down a sandwich. Her small circle of friends might wonder where she was, so she wrote some brief letters with a promise to be in touch to explain the reason for her sudden departure. Having contributed little to the running of the travel agents, the office would have no trouble in replacing her, and would need only a brief call next morning. After that, she must confirm that the cottage near her parents was still available.

It was an immense relief to be in the safety of her brother's home. Despite her recent dreadful experiences, they had, at least, propelled her into leaving London sooner. Her decisions all felt right.

The sun was streaming through the window when Sophia woke the next day. A tap on the door and Serena, bearing a large tray, announced that she was to have breakfast in bed.

'What luxury,' she cried, casting an eye over scrambled egg, bacon, mushrooms and triangles of toast. 'You're spoiling me, Serena.'

'No trouble at all and look, we'd love you to stay two or three days to gain a bit of strength.'

'That would be perfect.'

Sophia felt warmed by their concern, but longed to be back in the countryside she loved. To feel grass under her feet, to ride in the woods and fields, not to mention being her own boss. She couldn't wait.

Six months had gone by since Sophia left London. Seeing how contented she was, her parents soon gave up trying to persuade her that leaving London, and her job, was not the best idea. Initially, Pat and Rupert wanted her to live at home again, but they were firmly put in their place.

'No, I need to be independent . . . but I'll see lots of you.'

Sophia quickly acquired a list of customers needing not only rooms re-decorated, but often help with colour schemes. Being reliable, tidy and honest, her reputation spread and she also made a number of new friends.

To now be a short drive from her parents meant, after work, she could pop round to check they were in good health. Sometimes people she did not know well or particularly warm to would be paying a visit, and to her great amusement, look with disapproval at this creature in paint-spattered overalls climbing out of a dusty little van and advancing towards the front door.

'Have you met my daughter?' would leave them speechless and Sophia suppressing laughter.

Now and again there would be an invitation to a party in London, and as Sophia loved dressing up, she would sometimes go. Her parents hoped she might meet a nice man on one of these occasions, but for the moment she was truly happy. Who wouldn't enjoy a life of wearing so many different hats: her work, giving friends supper in the little kitchen of her cottage, riding and feeling part of the changing seasons. Her old life seemed very remote.

Sophia enjoyed keeping in touch with the two particularly good friends she had made during the Season, though living different lives meant seeing less of each other. Sophia was therefore delighted to hear from Georgina who, with her fiancé, had recently taken on running a small market garden and livery stables.

'Come over for lunch and meet Brian.'

'I'd love that,' Sophia replied. 'How long is the drive to you?'

'It's about forty-five minutes, but look, we're passing your door on Sunday, so we'll pick you up.'

'I'll be at my parents' house. Look forward to seeing you. Bye till then.'

Sophia was ready and waiting the following weekend. Spot

on midday, a car drew up and out stepped a young man looking, Sophia thought, nothing like the sort of person she would have expected Georgina to be engaged to.

He opened the door for her, but without introducing himself, and simply said, 'Georgina's busy cooking.'

He seemed disinclined to talk, and Sophia was able to study him unnoticed. He was fleshy with little fat fingers and his mouth hung open slightly.

She was relieved when, after what seemed a longer journey than anticipated, they turned down a tree-lined drive. As they arrived, Georgina appeared, framed by a rather imposing front door. She gave Sophia a warm welcome and ushered her through to a large kitchen. Being fond of her food, she had looked forward to a proper Sunday lunch. Georgina, however, had clearly spent only about ten minutes on preparing the meal. Ham and a plain salad sat in readiness at each place and Sophia wondered what her friend could have been doing all morning. Conversation was awkward and after a pudding of tinned fruit salad, Sophia asked to use the bathroom.

'Upstairs, second door on the right,' said Georgina sharply.

Sophia felt like crying and desperately wished she had come in her own car. The invitation must have been carefully planned and Georgina was punishing her for she knew not what.

Returning to the kitchen, she did her best to remain calm having decided to confront Georgina and find out what was going on. She and Brian were having an animated discussion, but moved apart as she walked in. Before Sophia could open her mouth Georgina said, 'We're going to show you the garden, but we'll do the stables first. It's a bit of a way so we'll go in the car.'

Sophia was a little cheered as they left the house, but the feeling went abruptly as she was bundled roughly into the back seat.

As they drove down a muddy track in silence, Sophia wondered what had happened to the warm, amusing friend she had known in London. Coming to a stop in a large yard, she felt distinctly apprehensive. It contained about ten loose boxes and other buildings, behind lay fields stretching to the horizon. Sophia got out of the car and was led down a narrow path.

'This is my best loose box,' shouted Georgina, 'and you're going in it.'

They both pushed her through the door almost winding her.

'Lock her in, Brian. You'll get what's coming to you, Miss Shaw.'

'What are you doing? What have I done?' cried Sophia.

Not only was the door locked, the top and bottom had been bolted together and a window with grills provided the only light.

With a feeling of utter disbelief, Sophia sank down on the straw. Recovering her breath, she observed a bowl of feed. Her first rational thought was that somebody would arrive with a horse and she would then be released—or make her escape.

Yet again, Sophia looked at her watch to find that the hands had hardly moved. It felt like a whole day. Another fifteen minutes went by—then, the sound of a car. Sophia positioned herself by the door. Footsteps stopped outside and an envelope was pushed under. Her hand shook as she opened the letter. It contained four typed pages from Georgina of accusations which, apart from one, were untrue.

Sophia went into a state of shock when she remembered discovering that the invitation to her dance had not been sent. When eventually found under a cushion, it was too late, and a mistake for which she had apologised profusely. She had clearly not been forgiven. The final page was about a horse, considered to be dangerous, who would be put in the stable that night, and of course, bite and kick and quite possibly kill her, an unfortunate accident. What Georgina didn't know, however, was that Sophia had been brought up handling and riding ponies and horses since the age of six.

Carefully folding the letter, she zipped it into a compartment of her bag, the one possession that she had managed to hang on to. A tiny lifeline. Sophia sat in a daze, feeling more despondent than she ever had in her life. Suddenly, in the awful silence she became alert at the sound of footsteps and hooves. The door was opened and a large black horse went straight to his food.

After one mouthful, he was clearly aware of Sophia. He snorted, and showed the white of an eye. It helped to know his name as it was painted on one of the water buckets.

'It's alright, I'm not going to take your supper, Warrior.'

He seemed to understand and continued to eat. Sophia spent the rest of the daylight hours attempting to make friends with her stable companion, who was certainly not the biting, kicking beast suggested by Georgina. As darkness fell, the sound of footsteps filled her with anticipation. The top door was unlocked and Brian silently passed her a plate of baked beans and a small bottle of water.

'Please speak to me, Brian?' pleaded Sophia.

'Can't. Maybe tomorrow.'

His reply gave her a glimmer of hope.

The food was tepid and Sophia wished she had eaten more of the unappetising lunch. When the chance of getting away arose she would need to be as fit as possible and must accept any food offered, however nasty. She had taken note of the open fields behind the stables which, had she been a fast runner, might have provided an escape route. She would need to be ready to take any opportunity. Too tired to make more effort at befriending Warrior, Sophia, aware that horses are inclined to pace round their stable at night, lay under the manger and cried herself to sleep.

She was woken by Warrior walking round the box in expectation of being taken to his field. Sure that Brian would come fairly early, she must try to convince him that this dreadful situation was a complete mistake. After an hour's wait, the door was unlocked and opened. Brian pushed in a large wheelbarrow.

'Can I leave now?' she begged tearfully.

'No, you gotta muck out.'

In one swift movement he led Warrior out and she was once more locked in and alone.

Brian would have to collect the barrow so it was best to do as she was told and clean up, weak as she felt. It would put her in a better position to ask him to let her go. Refusing to move or speak would not be helpful.

Another two hours went by before footsteps returned. The top door opened and Brian stood there with a plate of baked beans.

'You must listen to me, Brian.'

'I'll lose my job here if she knows we've been talking.'

'Whatever Georgina has told you about me, it's not true. Please believe me.'

'I don't know anything. Just do what she says.' Brian looked down and Sophia realised he felt awkward about keeping her locked up. She had misjudged him; he was not a bad young man, but simply following orders. Georgina's fiancé he was certainly not.

'I'd do anything for a cup of tea,' Sophia pleaded.

'See what I can do.'

'Oh! Thank you, thank you.'

As Brian trudged away, Sophia sank to her knees and thanked God. It seemed unbelievable that not so long ago she had been wearing beautiful dresses and drinking champagne at parties and dances, and now just the thought of tea meant everything. She had so far taken her life for granted and vowed if she got away, never to do so again.

Over the next few days, Sophia became weaker and spent much of the day dozing and almost ceasing to care about her plight. She was losing track of time. Had she been here days, weeks or a month? She wondered constantly about her family, sometimes becoming angry with them. Why, oh why, hadn't the police found her?

Warrior was not in the loose box every night. At least she was saved mucking out, but missed his company and the warmth of his body. Brian had taken pity on her and found an old, moth-eaten blanket for the nights.

Once, alone in the silent darkness, Sophie thought she heard footsteps. Was Georgina out there, lurking in the shadows, looking like the evil witch in a fairy tale and hissing through rotten teeth? Sophia shivered and pulling the blanket tightly round her, waited for the reassuring sound of the dawn chorus. Only then could she safely let go and drift off to sleep.

She was starting to give up, to think of death and perhaps her body never being found. One night, feeling emotionally drained, she fell into a deep sleep and awoke with a start. It was early morning and a female voice was calling Warrior. Sophia dragged herself to the door. 'He's in here. I've been locked in.'

'It's Mary, his owner. What's going on?'

'You must get the key. I think it'll be in the tack room or office. Please hurry.'

The footsteps died away, returning after what seemed to Sophia a very long five minutes. Her feelings of elation in those moments was like a small, flickering flame which had suddenly been ignited within her.

The right key was eventually turned in the lock and a bewildered young woman came face to face with her horse and a very dishevelled Sophia.

'My God, what's happened to you?'

Sophia collapsed in her arms, unable to speak.

'I'm taking you home with me. We'll get you to the car and I'll pop Warrior into the field.'

As they drove past the house, a furious Georgina came out shouting. Sophia didn't care what she was saying. 'Drive on, drive on quickly,' she screamed.

Hardly able to believe her luck, Sophia offered up a silent prayer of thanks to the Almighty for her rescue, which seemed nothing short of a miracle. It was not far to Mary's home and Sophia, starting to feel incredibly tired, allowed herself to be helped into a lovely warm kitchen. Before putting the kettle on, Mary briefly explained that she had been on holiday, but returning a day early, had decided to have a ride before breakfast.

'I'm afraid I messed up your plans,' Sophia apologised.

'My dear girl, don't be ridiculous,' Mary replied, giving her a little hug. Settling her into a comfy chair with a large mug of tea, she went into another room and rang the police.

It was only an hour since Mary had discovered a terrified girl in her horse's stable, but already a look of calm had come over Sophia's face.

'I think you're too tired to talk much yet. Just give me your husband's—'

'I'm not married. Please, could you ring my parents?'

Mary gently covered Sophia with a soft blanket.

'You have a sleep and then we'll talk.'

'You're very kind, and thank you for bringing me here,' said Sophia before closing her eyes.

'It's the least I could do.'

Mary rang the number Sophia had written down.

'Is that Mr Shaw? Look, I've got your daughter here.'

Sounding shocked and bewildered, he answered, 'Oh my goodness, we thought she was in Scotland. Her friend, Georgina, arranged for Sophia to go to a retreat.'

'I'm afraid that never happened. It appears that she has been kept against her will in a stable. She looks rather unkempt, as you might imagine, but seems well.

Mary gave directions to the house with an assurance that their daughter would tell them everything when they arrived.

Rupert had given Mary a brief run down of what Georgina had led them to believe. There had been no reason to think that their daughter hadn't gone to a retreat in Scotland, so remote that there was no telephone, to recover from a difficult time in London.

'Your parents will be here as soon as possible,' Mary told Sophia, now awake and requesting another mug of delicious tea.

'You were actually in the stable for two weeks.'

'And thanks to you, Mary, not longer than that. What was she planning I wonder? That Georgina is a . . . I can't even find the words.'

'If it's any comfort,' Mary said, 'the police will be questioning her at this moment. They'll want to talk to you as soon as you feel up to it.'

Rupert and Pat Shaw arrived looking pale and confused, but were soon made to feel at home in Mary's sitting room where Sophia, enjoying the comfort of a big sofa, told them as much of her ordeal as her energy would allow.

She was particularly anxious that Brian should not be punished too severely.

'He was good to me, really he was. It was just that he was petrified of Georgina and didn't want to lose his job.'

Having been quiet, Sophia's father spoke, 'I'm shocked to the core that we were completely taken in by that girl.'

'No, I can't believe it,' added her mother, who started rising to her feet.

'I think we should take you to the hospital now for a check-up, then home for rest and some jolly good meals.'

Once at the hospital, after a few minutes wait in a cubicle, a young doctor appeared, Sophia found him so charming she instantly felt better. He seemed slightly disbelieving, but intrigued by her story.

'Apart from losing a stone in weight, you're right as rain,' he told her.

Home, sweet home. As she walked through the front door, Sophia offered up another prayer of thanks. The telephone was ringing.

'I'll answer,' volunteered Pat, having guessed the identity of the caller.

'I know you want to talk to my daughter, but please give her time for some lunch and a rest.'

'Very well, Mrs Shaw, we'll be with you at 2.30.'

Sophia found the police officer kind and sympathetic, though she felt too weary to make much sense. She attempted to explain Brian's position.

'Georgina treated him very badly. He's a vulnerable person and she took advantage of that.'

'This is a serious incident we're dealing with, but I'll speak to one of my superiors. Try not to worry.'

Later on that day, after yet another sleep on a blissfully comfortable bed, Sophia rang Mary to thank her for all her help and kindness and a promise to keep her in the picture.

As a strong young woman, Sophia rapidly regained her strength, but was plagued with recurrent nightmares. In two days' time, Daniel would be arriving for the weekend and she needed to talk.

Putting the finishing touches to a cake on Friday afternoon, Sophia heard the sound of a car and rushed to the front door.

'Am I pleased to see you, my lovely brother. Come and sit in the kitchen and have some tea.'

'I feel awful, Sophia, I knew something wasn't right, as did some of your friends in London. I'm so sorry, I should have followed my instincts.'

'Don't feel bad about it, Daniel. Let's be thankful that Mum and Pop fell for Georgina's story. The anxiety would have made them ill.'

'Of course, it was her stalking you in London,' added Daniel.

Sophia then handed him the letter Georgina had written to her for comments.

'It's mainly lists of dates when you were late or didn't turn up, but I do think the girl needs treatment.'

'Do you think I do too?' enquired Sophia.

'Only if you feel the need to talk things through. You're a strong person and you will get over it.'

'You always allow me to let off steam, so I don't feel the need for professional help. You're a gem.'

Daniel quite suddenly asked, 'Would you like to go to America with me? I can organise it in no time.'

By Sunday, Sophia had decided definitely that, rather than talking to a counsellor, it would be best to get right away. What's more, she was free to leave at any time. She could speak to the police on her return, but in the meantime had been told that if Georgina pleaded guilty she would be sentenced to a year in prison. Sophia was thankful that Brian was now out of her clutches.

Sophia's parents had thoughtfully contacted her already concerned customers, nearly all of whom were happy to wait. With no word from the men in her life, the timing for going away was perfect.

The excitement of flying off to the States brought on a desire to give a party at her parents' home where there was plenty of room. It provided Sophia with a great deal to think about. In fact, her mind was so fully occupied she now dreamt of puddings rather than waking in a state from a nightmare.

The evening of the party arrived and all was ready for Sophia to greet her guests. She had a last minute panic that nobody would turn up, but like bees, a sudden swarm appeared. Rupert and Pat took on introductions and handed round drinks while she waited by the door for Caroline and her husband, Bruce, who had rung two days before to ask whether they could bring a friend. Hearing laughter in the background, she wondered if it might be someone she knew.

She started to worry when the telephone rang, but was

relieved to hear Caroline. They had got lost and would be a bit late. She hovered anxiously, wanting to give the couple and their friend a warm welcome.

When she opened the door to them a male figure was standing behind, but stepped forward sweeping Sophia into his arms. It was Nigel.

'What a wonderful surprise,' she managed, having had the breath squeezed out of her.

'And it's so lovely to see you again, Sophia.'

'I'd better circulate a bit and then we'll talk.'

At last they were able to sit together.

'There's so much to say,' they said in unison.

'But Nigel, thing is, I haven't contacted you because I heard you'd got a permanent girlfriend.'

'No, no,' Nigel replied without hesitation, 'it didn't last. Anyway, I thought you were spoken for.'

'Definitely not,' Sophia replied. 'You do need to understand that I'm not the same person you knew in London. When I get back from the States, I'll explain everything.'

'Can't wait,' said Nigel. 'I think you're fabulous and always will.'

Two days later, Sophia and Daniel left for California. Now, not only was she looking forward to going away, but even more to coming back.

After twelve years of marriage, it seemed to Sophia that she was reasonably contented. Nigel's proposal had not been especially exciting or romantic, but she had accepted, though very fond of him, out of a need for security. She knew he loved her and was dependable. They both took pride and delight in their children, Tancred and Cordelia.

One evening, Sophia's usual routine came to an abrupt end when Nigel arrived home and announced that he would be spending four nights a week in London. Sophia stood dazed and shocked for a moment, before running upstairs. How could he abandon her? How could he, she thought before sinking onto the bed.

Nigel found her sitting still as a statue.

'Why are you doing this?' Sophia asked, looking straight through him.

He sat and put an arm round her.

'I'm very sorry, Sophia. I'd been putting off telling you.'

He explained, at some length, that he would not get promotion, nor an increase in salary, if he didn't spend more time in the office.

'I want to do the best for my family.'

'I do understand.' Sophia knew it was hopeless to argue as clearly all the arrangements had been made. He had even rented a small flat in London.

The summer holidays were almost upon them. Sophia thought eight weeks too long and the idea of having no companionship in the evenings filled her with gloom.

On the Sunday before starting his new routine, Nigel mentioned he'd been in touch with the local dog rescue centre. Would Sophia go on Monday to see a black Labrador bitch needing a home?

The children were beside themselves with excitement. Sophia was touched by Nigel's thoughtfulness and knew a dog would give them all a sense of purpose.

Lovage, the name decided on for their new friend, was duly collected and taken to her new home. She seemed nervous to start with, but the children were gentle creatures and Sophia was confident all would be well and that Lovage would quickly adapt to her new surroundings and family.

Despite the demands and friendship of a dog, Sophia still missed Nigel's company and found the evenings lonely.

One afternoon the telephone rang. It was her old friend Caroline. Sophia's spirits instantly lifted.

'I haven't heard from you for ages. Tell me your news?' asked Sophia eagerly.

Caroline had apparently moved and was not far away. Sophia, the children and the dog were invited for a day the following week. A lovely end-of-holiday treat.

It was a prayer answered as far as Sophia was concerned and a comfort to know her friend was within easy reach. She had little idea then of just how much she was going to need her.

On the morning of their visit to Caroline, Sophia watched her children collect toys, books, woollies and wellies. Even her Morris Traveller had an expectant look as everything was stowed away with great enthusiasm. Finally, Lovage jumped in the back and they were off.

Caroline's new home was a long, low cottage with a big garden. She was waiting at the front door holding the hand of her daughter, Dolly. After greetings the children ran off to play leaving the friends to talk. As soon as Caroline asked after Nigel, Sophia confided how upset she was to be left holding the fort for four days a week while Nigel put his feet up in the London flat. In addition to this, Sophia went on, he seemed reluctant to spend time with his family during the weekends.

'Look Sophia,' Caroline said sternly, 'I've got friends who are left five nights a week. Nigel clearly sees it as his duty to look after you all. And what are these weekend activities you're not included in?'

'Well, he often plays golf. I don't understand people who enjoy chasing round after a little white ball.'

'All sounds harmless enough. He needs his relaxation.' Caroline noticed tears welling up in Sophia's eyes.

'Oh, I'm so sorry. I really didn't mean to upset you.'

'No, no. I'm fine and needed that talking to.'

After a tour of the cottage, Sophia was able to give Caroline some ideas on colour schemes. It gave her great pleasure to make a useful contribution.

A little later than planned, Sophia, the children and dog were rounded up to return home.

About a dozen miles into their journey, Sophia knew the engine didn't sound right. Sure enough, with a final splutter the car stopped. The country was open with not a house in sight. Nowhere to make a telephone call. There was nothing for it but to take a chance and flag down any passing vehicle.

Having taken Lovage for two walks along the grass verge, the children were starting to look worried. 'Will we have to sleep in the car, Mummy?' asked Cordelia.

'Somebody will come along, don't worry,' answered Sophia sounding more confident than she felt.

'And I'm hungry,' added Tancred.

It had already been forty minutes and not a sight or sound of life. Sophia's mouth had gone dry with anxiety. Another half an hour went by. Nigel would be ringing during the evening and, getting no answer would, Sophia knew, be very concerned, but what could she do? While working her way through these thoughts, oh joy, the sound of a car. Sophia leapt out of the Traveller and started waving frantically. An elderly lady stopped and wound down the window.

'Can I help?'

'Yes, please,' answered a relieved Sophia.

Having explained their situation, the good Samaritan drove off with a wave and a promise to get someone from the garage, a few miles on, to come out. She seemed, Sophia felt sliding back into her seat, a pretty trustworthy person.

True to her word, it was not long before a van, bearing the name Ned's Garage drew up behind them.

'What's the trouble?' a young man asked as he lifted the bonnet.

'You tell me,' Sophia answered a little irritated.

After a good look at the engine he delivered the bad news.

'I'll have to come back tomorrow and tow her to the garage.'

'Oh dear, what are we supposed to do?'

'I'll have to take you all home in the van.'

By moving tools and some oily rags, Cordelia and her brother were squeezed into the back along with a somewhat reluctant dog.

'By the way, I'm Mick. Give me directions to your house as we go along.'

Sophia introduced herself and apologised for seeming ungrateful.

'That's OK,' Mick turned towards her, smiling and showing a row of beautiful white teeth. 'You'll be alright now,' he added soothingly.

Mick dropped a by then rather weary family back at the house with a promise to return a good-as-new vehicle very soon.

The telephone was ringing as they stepped through the front door. Nigel had become increasingly concerned when Sophia failed to answer the telephone at the usual time. She explained briefly about the breakdown and he sounded relieved that they were all in one piece.

With the children safely in bed, Sophia settled on the sofa with a glass of wine and reflected on the eventful day. She was a little disturbed to find herself intrigued by Mick.

The following weekend Sophia knew Nigel was certain to question her again about the breakdown. However, having braced herself for an interrogation, he merely made a suggestion.

'You should get rid of that car.'

Sophia was relieved but hurt. 'Certainly not, it's part of the family.'

On Monday morning, as hoped, Mick swept into the drive in a shining Morris Traveller.

'Going like a dream now. Gave her a wash too. Do you mind dropping me back at work?'

'Of course I will, but would you stay at the wheel? I'm worn out getting the children organised.'

Sophia had looked forward to the half-hour drive as an opportunity of finding out more about Mick. She had a knack for extracting information from people and he was soon telling her about Doreen, his wife. He had hoped to start a family after a couple of years, but had now been married for six. His voice became a little shaky when talking about how much he longed for children.

'Have you always lived in this area?' ventured Sophia not wishing him to become too emotional at this stage and recognising the signs of someone wanting to confide in her.

'I lived on an estate not far from here. My dad was the gamekeeper. He was wonderful. He taught me all about the countryside and wildlife.'

Mick was clearly very proud of his knowledge and keen to share it. Sophia suspected he was more than a pair of greasy hands under the bonnet of a car.

'The school could use someone like you next term,' Sophia suggested.

'I've got a bit of time on Wednesday afternoons.' Mick seemed enthusiastic and sounded confident about the idea of sharing his knowledge of birds and wild flowers.

'OK. I'll have a word with the headmistress this afternoon. She won't mind me popping in to see her at home.'

Sophia drove away feeling very pleased with herself.

Having secured a few minutes of the headmistress's time, the response to Sophia's suggestion left her feeling deflated and rather foolish.

'Our nature study is catered for, thank you, Mrs Bacton.' There was no means of contacting Mick to pass on this message apart from ringing the garage. The receptionist would not understand, so her only option was to book in for a rather early service.

After some hesitation, Sophia put through a call to the garage.

'I'd like Mick to service my Morris Traveller, please.'

'He's ever so busy,' a crisp female voice answered. 'Hold on and I'll find out.'

After what seemed at least half an hour's wait, Sophia could hear high heels clicking on the concrete floor. 'Bring it in Thursday, ten o'clock.'

Three days later, Sophia swung into the little customer car park and made her way to the workshop. A pair of legs stuck out from beneath a car.

'Hello,' she called through the blare of a dusty radio. The rest of the body emerged.

'I've left the car and I need a lift home, please.'

'OK, give me a few minutes.'

As they drove, Mick was quiet. Sophia took a deep breath.

'I'm sorry, Mick, the school doesn't seem to need anyone.'

'Well, I'm not sure they'd want the likes of me.' After another long silence Mick said, 'Tell you what, bring the children to the big car park by the common Wednesday afternoon, 3.30, and I'll tell them about plants and butterflies—whatever they want to know.'

'Oh, they'd love that. I'll bring a thermos and sandwiches and biscuits—homemade, of course.'

Mick flashed his beautiful white-toothed smile. It never failed to charm her.

That evening, sitting with her customary glass of wine, Sophia realised the children would tell their father about Mick.

If some school friends joined them it would be more acceptable; she could tell him over the telephone that evening.

There seemed no apparent reason why she should feel guilty, but she did.

At breakfast the next morning, Sophia suggested the children should each invite a friend for the walk and picnic. The idea was readily accepted. Hardly liking to admit it to herself, she realised the outing provided an excuse for her to see Mick. Each time a wave of guilt hit her, she reminded herself of the benefits the children would reap. She prepared herself for a run down of the week which Nigel would expect.

As predicted, he asked Sophia about their activities. She told him how excited the children were about the walk with Mick. He made no comment but disappeared into his study. Sophia's stomach did a somersault.

Later that evening, Nigel reappeared. Sophia, busy chopping vegetables, felt his eyes on her.

'By the way,' he said, 'why are you taking your car to this young man? What's wrong with the local garage?'

'Nothing, but he does do an exceptionally good job. It's never gone better since the breakdown.'

'All I'll say is just watch the bills.'

Sophia was so relieved she abandoned the chopping and gave him a hug.

'I've got something to tell you,' she said. 'Quite soon I'll be able to pay some of my own bills.'

'How come?' asked Nigel.

'Well, two friends and I are starting a catering business. We've been planning it for a while.'

'Sounds like a splendid idea, Sofe.'

Nigel was a generous man at heart, a hunter-gatherer, prepared to bear food to the cave whenever necessary. Although he enjoyed providing the family with all their financial needs, he knew better than to put a stop to her cookery project. He admired her enterprise, indeed everything about her. For reasons he couldn't work out, he seemed unable to express it in words. She probably found him pompous at times. How he longed to let go and be more relaxed.

Wednesday afternoon was a bright and sunny one. Sophia and the children waited in the car park as arranged. It was after 3.30—perhaps he wouldn't turn up. Despite being a country girl, her knowledge of nature didn't extend much beyond buttercups and daisies. Suddenly, all heads turned to the entrance when the loud roar of a motorbike announced Mick's arrival. He raised his hand and wheeled the machine over. After much questioning by the boys, he persuaded the group to follow him.

Sophia brought up the rear and studied him from behind. He was tall and slim and wore tight blue jeans and a leather jacket. His blond hair was boyishly untidy. It was quickly apparent that he had an affinity with children, cleverly combining names of birds and flowers with games of hide and seek.

The picnic and whole afternoon were a great success.

Such was their enthusiasm, Mick was persuaded by the children to meet them regularly. Word spread quickly and the group increased in size.

The following term, high marks were achieved in the school nature class thanks to Mick and to the great annoyance of the headmistress.

Sophia started making regular trips to the garage in Mick's dinner hour. They would go round the back and sit on a rug, weather permitting. Sophia laughed when he always produced either ham and pickle or cheese and pickle sandwiches.

'I'm sure we could do better than that,' she commented one day. 'You know I'm involved with catering now? Well I'm going to bring some leftovers from the buffets for you.'

Mick looked uncertain about the offer.

'Don't worry, you'll enjoy some different foods.'

Now knowing him better, Sophia had gradually been able to draw him out on his times of preoccupation. His desire to have children was in danger of becoming an obsession. Doreen liked the idea of a family, but had become terrified of giving birth, her friends having apparently regaled her with stories of the unbearable pain and of all the possible complications. This inevitably meant that bedroom activity suffered. Mick was very grateful to have someone to talk to.

Over the next few weeks, Sophia evolved a plan. It was one fraught with complications and needing extremely sensitive handling. Those involved would have to be totally discreet.

One beautiful afternoon when they had an opportunity of meeting for a walk, Sophia was unusually quiet.

'What's up, Sofe?' asked Mick.

'OK, I've had an idea.' She became quiet again.

'Come on, spit it out.'

'Well . . . because I'm pretty sure I'm still fertile as a rabbit, Mick.'

He laughed.

'I could have a baby for you.'

'Do what?'

He started walking away from her. My goodness, what have I done, thought Sophia, and wished she hadn't spoken.

She caught up with him. He was sitting on a little hillock.

'I'm sorry—' she started. He then turned towards her. He had tears in his eyes.

'That's the best thing anyone's ever said to me.'

They held each other tightly. 'Listen, Mick, there's a huge amount to think about.'

'It means we'll have to—you know.'

'Well, that's what people usually do,' Sophia laughed.

'I'll be ever so nervous,' said Mick.

'No, you won't. It'll be all about creating your child. What I need to say though is this mustn't become an affair. There'll be enough problems without that and I want to keep my marriage intact. I'm sure you understand.'

'Of course,' he nodded.

Next time they met, Sophia told Mick about a friend who did beauty treatments for her and also fostered babies. The child would be well looked after by Fenella until such time as the adoption could go ahead.

'Hey, what about this as an idea, Mick? I could be his or her godmother.'

'Not sure about that. I don't even go to church.'

'Give it a try. Why not?' suggested Sophia.

'I'll think about it.' Mick would go no further.

'Perhaps I should meet Doreen.' She quickly realised in her excitement that thoughts were getting a little out of control and added. 'No, that would be unwise.'

Sophia was to give Mick some notice before their 'get together' so that he could take the afternoon off. To start with Mick felt anxious and unsure and had moments when he wondered if this was the right way forward, rather than going down the usual adoption channels. With a surge of optimism, however, he was soon thrilled at the idea of this small person, his own flesh and blood, a special gift for he and Doreen.

During the following days, there were many times when Sophia too wondered what on earth she was doing, but felt compelled to carry through the plan. She would not go back on her word.

When starting to feel queasy in the mornings, her feelings were mixed. She had gone through a time of hoping she wasn't pregnant, Mick was keeping his distance and she felt very alone.

Not far into the pregnancy, Caroline was coming over to lunch and Sophia looked forward to her company.

Though an effort, she had prepared a simple cold meal. Having exchanged family news, she was aware of her friend observing her closely.

'Sofe, you're only picking at your food. Not like you at all.'

'I'm well, thanks, Caroline.'

'You're not . . . are you?'

Having sworn her friend to secrecy, the story of Mick poured forth. Caroline listened attentively.

'My dear girl, I'm not sure if you're completely insane or very brave, but I'll support you in every way I can.'

'I'm so grateful 'cos I haven't been able to talk to anyone. I'll tell Nigel once the morning sickness is over.'

'We'll make some arrangements together soon and you just ring any time you feel the need,' Caroline assured her.

A huge weight lifted from Sophia, who badly needed someone trustworthy to help her make plans. 'I couldn't ask for a better friend than you, Caroline.'

Nigel, at home the following weekend, had noticed Sophia looked pale and was quieter than usual.

'Anything the matter, Sofe?' he enquired.

She was taken completely by surprise and decided this might be the very moment to tell Nigel about the pregnancy.

'I wasn't planning to tell you yet, but I'm pregnant.'

'Sorry, I didn't quite—'

'You heard . . . we never planned to have any more. Must have forgotten to take the pill. Anyway, I'm not happy about it,' answered Sophia. Lying did not come easily and she wanted to sink through the floor.

'You mean you want an abortion?' Nigel shouted at her.

'No, no. He or she could be adopted.'

'I suppose it's your choice. What will people think . . . What will they say?'

'I don't show much so no one will notice. Anyway, it's nobody else's business,' said an unusually defensive Sophia.

'I despair of you,' Nigel suddenly left the room, slamming the door behind him.

For once Sophia was relieved when Monday morning came and Nigel would be returning to London. They had barely spoken since telling him about the baby. The last thing she wanted was to jeopardise her marriage through her perhaps mistaken generosity to another couple; she feared she may have done just that.

'What's done is done,' said Caroline on the telephone later that day.

'I think you'll find Nigel will calm down. Give him time.'

'I'm sure you're right,' Sophia replied, 'but I've never seen him so upset and angry. How do I cope with the months ahead?'

'You'll be fine. Just take care of yourself and be positive. This baby is your priority now.'

Sophia was relieved to speak to Caroline with her down-to-earth approach to life.

It was too soon to explain to Cordelia and her brother about the baby's adoption. Being untruthful about the reason filled her with shame, but it was her only choice. She had to find the courage to talk to the children soon. Caroline, she knew, would tell her to just get on with it. Fortunately, with much of their time devoted to home work and also to the school's drama and dance groups, Sophia was able to rest quietly. Her great fear was that Nigel might say something to the children in anger. His nightly telephone calls were brief and not very friendly. She braced herself for Friday and his return.

Nigel's days were busy with work, but he dreaded the evenings in his small flat. He had been completely bewildered and hurt by Sophia's news. He failed to understand her attitude and was shocked that she wanted the baby adopted. It was so out of character. For the moment, he could think of nothing appropriate to say, but still loved her deeply.

Rather than being distant and aloof, Sophia welcomed Nigel home the following weekend and, having put his favourite supper on the table, found him gentle and thoughtful. Sophia desperately hoped things would continue in this way.

On Sunday afternoon, hoping Nigel might have come to terms with the idea of the child being adopted, she was completely taken aback when he announced that not only was he returning to London, but would not be coming home for the foreseeable future.

'If you need anything, you can ring my secretary.'

Sophia was plunged into gloom. She only had herself to blame and would just have to manage.

As soon as he opened his mouth, Nigel regretted telling her to leave messages for him via his secretary. What was he doing suggesting Miss Cooper act as a go between? Fortunately, he had never actually asked her and now his anger had subsided, the idea of not even speaking to Sophia was unbearable. Lines of communication must be kept open and he would ring that evening from the flat. Being unable to face seeing her changing body, he would still stick to his decision to stay away until after the birth and adoption of the child. Only then could he return to be with the woman he loved.

It transpired, when talking to Cordelia later, that her father had rented a bigger flat so that she and Tancred could stay with him in London for theatres and museum visits.

While not relishing the idea of an even more silent house, Sophia was pleased for them. Their horizons would be widened.

Caroline kept in close touch and she and Sophia were able to discuss any problems that arose. During their next call, Sophia put her in the picture over what was happening.

'It would be extraordinary if Nigel wasn't confused and hurt. Incidentally, I'll never regret getting you two back together at that party you gave all those years ago. He absolutely adores you; he's a good man.'

Caroline's little speech was very welcome and gave Sophia a warm feeling.

'Keep your chin up, at least you have that dog keeping a beady eye on you.'

'Yes,' answered Sophia, 'I'm incredibly lucky to have such a loyal and loving companion, but it's becoming difficult to give her the time she deserves.'

During the following week, Mick rang promising more support from now on, and reading her thoughts, made an offer to look after Loveage. With an uncertain and difficult time ahead, Sophia was grateful and accepted. She would miss the companionship, but knowing Mick had been brought up with animals, a good home was certain.

This difficult decision forced Sophia to tell Tancred and Cordelia, not only that Loveage would be leaving to be with another family, but also about the expected baby. They not only took the news of the baby in their stride, but made it clear that after their school activities and friends were as important.

She did her best to explain what was to happen after the

birth. The children were clearly upset about their dog, but more so for their mother.

'Perhaps she could come back when things get easier,' suggested Tancred.

'We'll see,' Sophia smiled putting an arm round both of them.

Sophia was starting to feel more optimistic, especially now Caroline had devised a plan. She would give birth in the local maternity home, followed by two days at her friend's house.

Sophia couldn't help feeling anxious about the little one's future, but simply had to trust those involved with the adoption. As well as keeping as healthy as possible, she spent time preparing herself mentally for the separation from her child.

One Friday about a month after the birth, Nigel arrived home sooner than Sophia expected, and looking very despondent. Her heart rate increased instantly. Perhaps he had somehow found out about Mick. She followed him into the sitting room where he sat down heavily and asked her to join him.

'I've got something to tell you. I saw the doctor yesterday, I've got angina and other complications and I feel pretty rotten.'

Sophia burst into tears.

'Please don't cry.'

'I can't help it. I feel so awful,' sobbed Sophia.

'Don't be silly. It's hardly your fault.'

That evening they talked more than they had for a long time. Sophia realised how deeply she cared for her husband and would cherish and look after him until the end of his life.

Angela was now four months old and after much discussion, Sophia and Mick agreed she should be godmother. The reason for choosing her, it was explained to Doreen, was that Sophia had been especially helpful with two useful introductions, both of which had secured his new job as manager of a smart new car showroom. Doreen was delighted by the choice as Sophia was posh and therefore probably rich. Exciting, expensive presents for their little girl? She couldn't wait to tell her girlfriends over coffee on the Wednesday morning.

Their attendance at church services had not been as good as hoped. However, Mick conscientiously kept the churchyard meticulously tidy and impressed the vicar with his knowledge of birds spotted there. Working with his hands was one way he could show his gratitude for Sophia's gift of his precious baby. No expense would be spared on a party in the hall after the christening.

Sophia saw less of Mick since his promotion. Though still fond of him, she was not sure she cared for the way he now strutted about the showroom in a suit with slicked-back hair, persuading customers to part with rather more money than planned for a sleek new motor. She looked back nostalgically to visiting the friendly little garage, or taking off on his motorbike to have a picnic in the woods. Such joyous freedom.

She found it touching that Mick and Doreen had gone to such trouble and careful planning over the christening and party though, because Nigel was so unwell, she could not be away from him for long and left before the celebration in the hall. Angela was clearly deeply loved by her parents, and able to play her role as godmother, the future for the little girl looked rosy. Aware of the joy she had brought two people, Sophia offered up a prayer of thanks before going home to a man who needed her comfort and love.

Fewer family responsibilities allowed Sophia to put her energies into caring for Nigel and their final years together were the closest they had ever been.

After his death, Sophia discovered that, being the husband that he was, Nigel had saved and invested money for her widowhood. She had no wish to remain permanently in their family home, but had decided to stay until after Angela left school.

Life seemed to be simply ticking over as she grieved, but she was, over the next few years, gradually drawn back to her interests and hobbies, and to her great joy, met a young woman looking for someone to share a horse. Just what was needed to take her out of herself. Fortunately, Nina the owner had suggested a trial period and after a few rides, there was simply no rapport between horse and rider. Though a disappointment, it had the effect of giving Sophia a nudge towards thoughts of the immediate future.

The house, now more suited to a young family, should go on the market, but the priority was a farewell party for friends who had shown great kindness to her family combined with Angela's eighteenth birthday celebration. A farewell surprise for her before leaving to start her nurse's training in London. Plans needed to be made immediately.

Sophia loved nothing more than arranging a party, but felt sad and uncomfortable at the thought of it being Angela's eighteenth in Nigel's old home. He had buried the pain of the birth by never speaking of her. In turn, Sophia guessed his feelings and hid her acute guilt. It was something she had to live with. Never in a million years would she have put the burden of her secret on Nigel's shoulders. As a wise friend once said, 'Don't dump your pain onto someone just to make yourself feel better.' Pushing these thoughts away, she must try and live in the moment.

The evening of the party was suddenly upon her with everything ready for a wonderful time. Family and friends, all able to come, gave Sophia particular pleasure since, very shortly, she would be on the road to begin the search for her dream cottage.

One memory of the evening would be forever fixed in her mind. Standing at the entrance to the marquee and aware of Mick by her side, with Doreen a little behind, a circle of young people suddenly parted revealing a dazzling creature. It was as though Sophia was looking at her young self. Angela wore a stunning turquoise dress with her blond hair thick and shining like an aura. Seeing them, she ran over and gave Mick and Doreen a hug and then Sophia, pressing an envelope into her hand.

Only when she crawled into bed at 2 am did Sophia allow herself to open Angela's card. It expressed her thanks and love, and inside were seven beautifully drawn magpies. She recalled how they would joke about one for sorrow, two for joy, but seven for a secret never to be told. 'My goodness, she knows.'

Sophia treated herself to a lie in the next morning. Looking again at the card, she decided that for the time being she would say nothing. Angela had plenty to think about before leaving for London.

The house sold quickly, though for less than hoped. After sorting items to go into storage, Sophia allowed herself only the minimum of clothes and possessions, because until she found her cosy cottage, home would be a camper van. Mick seemed greatly amused by this acquisition.

'Why haven't you bought yourself a Triumph Stag or something?' he asked.

'Completely impractical,' answered Sophia. 'I want to be nomadic for a while and I never need bother friends to make up a bed for me.'

'You are a one,' Mick shook his head. 'Just an old gypsy aren't you?'

'Not so much of the old, but yes, I think I am.'

At their last meeting, Mick gave the camper van a final check and handed Sophia some photographs. Each one celebrated a birthday, right up to Angela's eighteenth. They would be much treasured possessions.

'I will put pen to paper and use the showroom address, of course,' Sophia told him as she started to move off.

Mick didn't reckon on writing letters, so he simply smiled showing his still beautiful white teeth and waved her goodbye.

Henry was a man who took his responsibilities very seriously and persuading the people in his life that he needed a short break away had not been easy.

It was a sunny autumn afternoon and, as he sat in his much loved old 4x4 preparing to leave, he was aware of a feeling of unease. He took a deep breath and started his journey.

Some twenty miles away, Sophia was waiting in a car park. She had arrived early and brought a newspaper to fill in the time. Butterflies played havoc with her stomach, preventing her from taking in a single word. After what seemed an eternity she left her car to wait at the appointed place.

As Henry turned into the car park, any feelings of doubt melted away as soon as he saw Sophia. She was wearing a brown skirt and green jersey and looked, Henry thought, like a delicious nut fallen from a tree. They embraced briefly and he stowed her luggage in the back.

After enquiring about each other's health and well-being, they were silent as this was a completely new departure from the way they usually met.

Henry had been looking for someone to give advice on his rather wild garden. When he heard from friends about Sophia's natural aptitude for garden design, plus a very good eye for interiors, he decided she was just the person he needed.

When they made contact, she was quick to point out that she

had no formal qualifications, but was always pleased to make suggestions. He understood that, while not accepting money, those she helped would show their appreciation with gifts. He had therefore given her a number of small presents. One day he announced that he was going to take her somewhere as a special thank you. Sophia could not resist this intriguing invitation.

Henry broke the silence by putting an Ordnance Survey map on her lap and giving her arm a pat.

'As someone from an Army family, are you okay with that?' he asked.

'Er . . . yes' she answered, unwilling to admit to not having looked at one for a long time and certainly not since the convenience of Sat Nav. 'Anyway, I see we're going to Wales. How lovely, and absolutely one of my favourite areas.'

Her enthusiasm made Henry smile as he had planned this trip meticulously and was now confident it was going to be a great success. She blew a kiss in his direction as if to confirm.

Darkness was falling when they turned off the main road into a thickly wooded area. An owl swooped across in front of them, off for a night of feasting and flirtation.

Henry's sense of adventure was building up as he passed Sophia the torch.

'When the time comes, I've marked the grid references for you and we're heading for Berry Farm.'

It started to rain making the tarmac glisten in the headlights. Gusts of wind sent twigs swirling and banging on the windscreen, but before long, they left the woods behind, the weather cleared and they were able to see the occasional twinkling light of a cottage or small farm. The roads became one-track lanes with a line of moss in the middle indicating a less populated area. The terrain changed again and Sophia was aware of some sheer drops to her left. She disliked heights, but decided that should they tip over the edge, at least she would be with Henry.

He sensed her tension and asked, 'Alright, sweetie? It shouldn't be far so have a look at the route.'

He was now skilfully negotiating hairpin bends and Sophia prayed she wouldn't feel queasy.

'Okay,' she said, 'next left and immediately right up a hill and the farm is on the left. I see there's a lot of mixed woodland.'

She felt rather pleased with this observation. It wasn't long before a reflective light on a post indicated their destination had been reached and straight ahead a bumpy track led to a large clearing. Sophia gasped with childlike pleasure.

'A beautiful log cabin, I've always wanted to stay in one. A dream comes true.'

Once inside the warmth and scent from a large wood burning stove welcomed them. They hugged each other tightly with affection as well as relief on their safe arrival after a difficult journey.

Apart from the living room, another door led into a tiny bathroom and next to it the only bedroom. Sophia had considered querying the sleeping arrangements, but was glad to have left it alone.

'I'm sure you will find it to your liking,' Henry told her, opening the door.

Instantly, her eye alighted on the bedspread, an exquisitely handmade patchwork quilt. It took Sophia back many years, to one Nigel's mother had lovingly stitched. Tancred and Cordelia would choose a patch at bedtime and be entertained by their mother's story of its history. Henry then spoiled her pleasure by tipping the entire, crumpled contents of his bag onto the bed.

'Do you call that unpacking? At least let me do some pressing for you.'

'That's sweet of you,' said Henry, 'but first there's no electricity here, and secondly I don't want you doing chores.'

'The paraffin lamps are so effective I keep forgetting,' said Sophia as she started neatly folding and transferring the garments onto a chair.

Quite suddenly, she felt weary and, because they were finely tuned into one another's needs and feelings, Henry suggested she should go and have a bath.

'I promise there is hot water. It comes from a boiler behind the stove,' he explained.

The bathroom was a little chilly, but fortunately Sophia was not a 'me time and candles' person, and when he appeared bearing a glass of wine for each of them, she was almost ready to get out. It felt completely natural and merely a gesture of his thoughtfulness that he held out a large blue towel in which to wrap her. Having hopped in himself, he returned to the bedroom to find her curled up like a cat and looking very drowsy.

Henry went and sat down in the living room and allowed his thoughts to wander. He was immensely grateful to have discovered this wonderful place. The three couples living and working at Berry Farm provided a unique experience for visitors. There were no computers, TVs or even a mobile phone network and consequently people apparently, rather than switching off were switched on to find their senses heightened. He had been a little anxious that Sophia might be out of her comfort zone, however, she appeared to be completely comfortable, zone and all. He thought about their first meeting and being aware of a force between them that was so strong it was like two magnets being drawn together with a click. He treasured their long talks following rather formal discussions concerning the house or garden, but was conscious of not being completely open because he felt strongly about keeping her separate from his sometimes profound anxieties.

His thoughts were interrupted by the tinkling of a bell on the veranda. On investigation he discovered food had been left. He carried it through to the kitchen and quickly laid the table.

At that moment, Sophia appeared looking much refreshed and they were soon eating delicious lamb followed by a colourful fruit salad.

Afterwards, they put on warm coats and sat outside by a chiminea, lit when the meal was delivered. Gazing up in wonder at the number and brightness of the stars, it was, Henry explained, because of far less light pollution in this part of the country.

'Your explanation does slightly spoil the romance,' laughed Sophia.

Not long after, she noticed Henry's eyelids beginning to droop and suggested they go and get better acquainted with the patchwork quilt.

'Good idea, Sophia. We've got a long and active day tomorrow.'

'I can't wait,' said Sophia, 'I love a surprise.'

In the early hours she was woken by a loud clap of thunder. She had no fear of the elements and positively enjoyed the winter when the wind and rain beat on the windows and she was cosily indoors. However, allowing herself to feel a little vulnerable, Henry put his strong, comforting arms round her.

Sophia next woke to sunshine streaming through the window and Henry standing by the bed holding a tray laid with a pretty china tea-set. No question of a mug plonked down on the table here. With a sweeping gesture, he presented her with a beautiful peach-coloured rose. He'd found it round the back where a bush was still stoically blooming into the colder weather.

'You are so thoughtful—thank you, dear heart,' said Sophia. 'What is the plan today?'

'Just get up in your jeans,' replied Henry, 'and a bit later on all will be revealed.'

Sophia produced scrambled eggs on a small camping stove and toast, using an elderly, long, three-pronged fork over the wood burner. After breakfast Henry disappeared and she sat down on a large floor cushion and sipped coffee. How well did she really know this man and was it a friendship or a relationship? She thought probably somewhere between the two. At times there would be an uncertainty about either when, on an apparent flip of a coin, he would withdraw and go away for a week, leaving her feeling anxious and puzzled. However, he would always return as though nothing had happened, and never volunteered any explanation. Instinct told her not to ask. Once together again, all was forgotten and forgiven. Henry was kind and considerate, humorous and always a delight to be with.

A noise outside and Henry calling her to the door galvanised her into action. Two horses were tied to the hitching rail; one a handsome liver chestnut and the other slightly smaller and stockier with distinctive markings. Sophia was with them in an instant, a hand on each soft nose. Henry then spotted an envelope attached to one of the saddles, apparently a note from the horses!

'Let's see what they say: "Dear visitors. We look forward to taking you out today. When you stop for a sandwich, we'd appreciate something to eat too. Small feed in saddle bag. By the way, I'm Gem, a Quarter horse, and my friend is Crystal, a Paint. Please get us home by 4 pm and don't forget to do the cinch up before you get on as you can't once in the saddle! With our love."'

'It's very trusting of the owner to let us go off on our own,' said Sophia.

'Don't worry,' explained Henry. 'They know you're an experienced rider and that I did a stint on a ranch. Anyway, come back in and we will get kitted out.'

Sure enough, a selection of Western riding gear hung just inside the door. Zipping herself into a pair of chaps, Sophia reminded Henry that the fringes were not originally decorative, but designed to disperse the rain.

'In case you thought I was just showing off,' she laughed. 'Come on, let's get going.'

Setting off down a narrow path, Sophia leading the way, Henry was perfectly positioned to admire her trim waist and

hips and decided it was quite difficult not to look elegant in a
Western saddle with its beautifully tooled leather and colourful
pad beneath. The path became a track and they could then ride
side by side. Gem and Crystal were clearly good friends, giving
each other a playful nip from time to time. Having anticipated
seeing interesting wildlife, Sophia and Henry were soon
rewarded by the sight of an adder coiled up, making the most
of a patch of autumn sun. As they passed it did not attempt to
slither away, knowing horses posed little threat.

Further into the woods they glimpsed deer, a stoat scuttling
across their path and red kites overhead.

The silence the pair had enjoyed for two hours was suddenly
broken by the sound of voices and barking. Round a corner
stood two boys and a dog. The taller one stepped forward
and held a hand up in greeting while the other commanded,
'Dillie—sit.'

'Where did you spring from?' enquired Henry.

Without answering the question he gave them an invitation.

'Would you like a cup of tea or something? Mum and Dad
would like to meet you.'

Exchanging puzzled looks, but curious, they followed the
boys and their blue merle collie and found themselves in a
clearing dominated by a large yurt.

'That's a Mongolian tent,' announced Henry, adding quietly,
'do you think this is part of the deal?'

'I suspect the horses have been here before, so let's just go
with it,' laughed Sophia.

A painted door then opened and a couple introduced
themselves as Martha and Colin and sons Ian and Gareth.

'Visitors from Berry Farm sometimes stop here for a rest,
but we don't see many people, so you are most welcome,' said
Colin. Then added, 'The boys will look after Crystal and Gem,
so come in.'

Inside, the yurt was colourful with plenty of seating. Two

stoves with chimneys taking the smoke out through the sides gave out just the right temperature.

Relaxing, after enjoying a packed lunch, Sophia and Henry were keen to find out about life in the woods. The family, they gathered, had a small arable farm a few miles away, but spent as much time as possible looking after six acres of woodland.

'Before you go, come and meet our two Welsh cobs. We use them for logging as much of the land is too steep for machinery. We also make walking sticks which we paint using various designs. You'll find a selection for sale at the farm, should you be interested.'

It was time to ride on if they were be back at the farm by 4 pm, so having admired the horses and thanked the family for their hospitality, Henry and Sophia went on their way.

'You won't get lost,' Colin called after them, 'the horses know every track and path and probably the time too!'

During their ride back, Henry took the chance of telling Sophia more about the organisation at the farm. Having studied leaflets sent beforehand, he was impressed enough to learn the information almost by heart. Sophia, although interested to know more, did think he sounded a little like a tour guide! Her final pleasure was seeing a butterfly, its wings moving a little, giving a message of beauty and peace. Probably the last she would see that year.

Alex, in charge of the horses, was waiting and enquired about their day.

'We've had a wonderful time and a lovely ride,' enthused Sophia as she got off and slid her hands under Crystal's mane—warm as a hot water bottle—before handing her over to join some other horses in the barn. A young woman appeared and introduced herself as Alex's wife. She pressed a box into Sophia's hands.

'A little something to keep you going.'

'Thank you,' said Sophia, 'no doubt another delicious treat.'

Walking back to the cabin, they agreed that there was an aura of harmony over the farm and woods.'

'Thing is,' said Henry, 'they work incredibly hard to create this atmosphere, using all their skills and gifts. I think visitors literally shed their stress at the gate.'

'It's certainly transmitted to the horses. They're so calm and happy,' added Sophia. 'I also know how vital meticulous planning is, 'cos as you know, I sometimes work for The Cool Catering Company and it's very satisfying when everything gels for a good party.'

Henry felt he should add that no one is perfect.

'I'm sure there is a certain amount of shouting and bickering, even here,' he smiled.

Settling down in front of the wood burner, they found the box contained a perfect cream tea. With the reward of food went a great sense of achievement and satisfaction since neither had been in the saddle for a while. Henry did, however, complain of stiff shoulders and back.

'Would you?' started Henry, raising an eyebrow.

'I know what you want. Yes, of course I'll give you a massage, but don't go to sleep 'cos my feet need some attention,' laughed Sophia.

This mutual giving of pleasure lulled them into a wonderful doze. Sophia then came to abruptly, remembering that she had brought a bottle of champagne. Henry was on his feet instantly.

'What a wonderful idea. I'll find some glasses.'

As they sipped and talked Sophia was aware of a familiar little grey cloud floating into her mind. Fortuitously, the bell was ringing outside to let them know supper had been delivered and the cloud dispersed. Henry had told her they were having lobster, and to do it justice she decided to change.

'Just going to glam up,' called Sophia disappearing to the bedroom. 'I'll be two minutes.'

Henry thought this most unlikely and decided ten to twenty

was nearer the mark. He admired the way she dressed. Everything about her was neat, except for her head which, seemed to him, a cocktail of creative ideas, feelings and emotions, the mix changing fairly frequently.

With a vision of colour returning from the bedroom, champagne and anticipation of delicious food, life couldn't get better, Henry decided.

While Sophia changed, she had made a brief plan of what she was going to say to Henry the following day, but was determined that their last evening should be happy and relaxed.

Waking later than they had meant, Henry said he would organise tea and toast. Sophia sensed an end of holiday atmosphere and felt she needed to be up, packed and getting ready to leave.

'There's something I need to do, and it'll take about forty minutes,' Henry clearly wanted her out of the way.

'That's fine,' said Sophia, 'I'll pop over to the farm.'

On the way to the house she passed a well-tended vegetable garden. It made her realise how you really tasted food here rather than simply eating it. Getting no answer to her knock, she went in and found herself in a small sitting room. A young woman was working at an old sewing machine while a handsome man sat with his feet on the fender.

'I'm so sorry to disturb your well-deserved relaxation,' said Sophia, 'we're off soon and I especially wanted to thank you for a unique experience, not to mention the delicious food.'

The young man was now on his feet.

'Sorry, we didn't hear the door; it's Penny's machine. Anyway, we love having people like you who appreciate what we're trying to do and thank you for choosing us.'

He gave Sophia a little bow as she left.

When she got back to the cabin, Henry had packed up and was awaiting her return. He had his hands behind his back.

'I've got something for you,' Sophia drew in her breath with surprise and pleasure as he presented her with a beautifully made miniature replica of the log cabin.

'You are amazing,' said Sophia. 'I'm thrilled with it. A thousand thanks, Henry.'

'I'm glad you weren't around when I was doing the finishing touches. It was very fiddly and my language got a bit out of hand,' he smiled.

Sophia volunteered to drive back allowing Henry to see the stunning countryside, but also to act as a diversion from an unpleasant sensation building up in her stomach. Nearing the main road, Henry, ever sensitive to Sophia's state of mind, asked, 'What's going on in that funny head of yours?'

'Oh nothing, nothing,' replied Sophia. 'I was thinking that there's probably nothing more I can help you with in the house and garden.'

'That's not what you were thinking at all,' replied Henry. 'I know there's something on your mind so I'm going to take you to this lovely pub, not too far from home. Incidentally, there's a post office next door if you want to collect your pension.'

'Thank you for thinking of that and I'd love to stop at the pub.' Thanks for reminding me of my age too, she thought.

As the pair continued the drive, they became subdued, but on reaching the pub their spirits lifted when finding a cosy, very private little corner. After some nourishment, Sophia felt able to open up.

'I feel I know everything but nothing about you,' she started, 'you've told me about Sarah, your sister, and how demanding she is, and I know you've got a son who lives abroad, but you never mention a wife. Why?'

'Alright, let's have a cup of coffee and I'll tell you.'

Sophia listened with a mixture of curiosity and horror to his story. He had been married to Joanna, a talented musician for thirty years. One night, he forgot to change a light bulb on the stairs and she fell, breaking numerous bones. Her recovery in hospital was slow and it was discovered that she had suffered some brain damage.

'You can imagine the almost unbearable guilt, although I still don't know why she wanted to go downstairs that night. Anyway, I did my best to look after her at home, but her mood swings became almost impossible. On bad days she blamed me continuously for the way she was, shouting, throwing food at me, you name it. Thank goodness her family supported both of us and decided she'd be better off in a home near her sister. I wasn't very good at coping with her physical or any other needs for that matter, and was probably heading for a nervous breakdown.'

'How long ago was the accident?' asked Sophia.

'Ten years ago,' he replied.

'I'm shattered by your story.'

Henry went on to tell her that he visited Joanna often and stayed nearby. 'When she is on an up,' he continued, 'she's her old self, wants to come home and talks of playing the oboe again.'

'You're in a very difficult position, and I'm so sorry.'

They continued their journey, Henry at the wheel this time. Sophia started to feel weak and her mouth had gone dry.

'You've no idea,' she started, 'how wonderful it was to spend some time with you in Wales. I'll remember it—always.' She felt tearful, but not wishing to spoil her carefully applied eye makeup, continued, 'I—'

'Yes, what?' queried Henry, starting to get tetchy. There seemed little point in continuing to talk until they had both calmed down, so they again drove in silence.

Not long after meeting Henry, Sophia began experiencing emotions which had laid dormant for years. It had knocked her sideways as she swung from anguish to happiness. Today, as someone who had just collected her old age pension, her feelings were still as intense as an eighteen-year-old.

Nigel had been dead for many years. Looking back, her love for him had been comfortable, built on friendship and trust. The difficult times had been mainly of her own making. Now, she was riding a dreadful roller coaster.

The car park where she had discreetly left her car beside a bush was now only five minutes away. She was not entirely sure why, but in her mind's eye she visualised her daughter, headmistress of a local school, giving her the 'go to the back of the class' look. Her son would merely raise his eyebrows. Neither of them knew she had been with Henry and she would simply say that she had enjoyed two days in Wales. Having located her car, Henry transferred her luggage and put the little log cabin carefully on the back seat.

'I feel its best, though it's not what I want, for us not to meet again.'

'Oh, for goodness sake,' said Henry again becoming defensive. 'You just came along for a good time. Right?'

'Please don't be like this,' Sophia's voice was becoming quite faint. 'I know I'm a coward and probably very selfish, but it all becomes too painful at times.'

Henry put his hand on her shoulder. 'I can't say I really understand you.'

'I'd better go,' Sophia whispered.

He sat for a moment and watched the tail lights of her car disappear, feeling despondent and disappointed that their three days together had ended in this way. He was grateful that she had spoken as she did, at least in the car park, therefore not spoiling their time of such joy and happiness. He did not care to analyse situations too much, and she had not made clear her reason for breaking off their contact. Perhaps he should not have told her about his problems, although at least she realised that Joanna knew nothing about her. I don't like the idea of being referred to as 'that women' Sophia had said.

Home seemed cold and unwelcoming so Henry quickly put the lights on and a match to the fire before listening to his messages and returning to reality.

There were three from his sister: 'You still haven't mended the chair or unblocked that upstairs basin. Why haven't I heard from you?' And two from the nursing home: 'Joanna is getting anxious, please ring.'

Henry had lived in his present house for five years. It had seemed sensible to move from a rambling old rectory to something more compact, but possible to adapt for Joanna should she return. Before he met Sophia the atmosphere had been rather gloomy, but for a modest investment, she had transformed it into a home. He found her colour schemes a bit over the top, so they compromised by visiting art galleries and buying pictures to provide interest. During the evening, Henry was able to reflect on the last three days. He was sure the memories would remain sharp for the rest of his life and sustain him when he needed it. In his heart he knew that whatever had been said by Sophia, it was not meant to be hurtful and that all would be well.

He and Sophia had shared many past experiences sitting at his kitchen table, and from time to time she had talked about the dreadful ordeal of being stalked and held against her will. It occurred to Henry that her uncharacteristic behaviour earlier that day might be old feelings resurfacing. She had mentioned that forming new female relationships was now more difficult, but nothing more specific. It transpired that Georgina was a complex psychopath, which meant that she would never have physically hurt Sophia. After treatment, about three years later, she had written a letter of apology for which Sophia was grateful.

Sophia got back into her car feeling very low. One of her jumbled thoughts was the realisation that her rejection of Henry was in fact her own fear of it. It was beginning to get dark, which gave a certain protection. She turned towards home and hadn't driven far, when she knew she had to stop. She spotted a lay-by sign and turned into it. Putting her head on the steering wheel she simply sobbed her heart out. Suddenly aware of headlights, a car pulled up immediately behind her. I could do without this, so just go away she thought, but was then aware of footsteps approaching and a light tap on the window. A tall, dark police officer stood there, obviously wanting to speak.

'Have I done something wrong?' she asked.

'No, but I noticed you a little way back looking a bit distressed and wondered if everything was okay with the vehicle.'

'Yes, I'm fine thanks, and so is the car.' She was grateful and rather touched by his concern. Another tear fell with a plop. He reached into his pocket and offered her a tissue.

'It is clean, madam.'

'I'm sure it is—thank you.'

As he stepped away he said, 'If you're sure you're alright, have a safe journey home and make yourself a nice cup of tea.'

'Thanks so much.'

With a little smile from Sophia he gave a salute and went on his way.

While needing to release emotions, Sophia was profoundly grateful that he had brought her back to reality. Her strong coping mechanism, built up over many years, was coming into play and she had an overwhelming desire to return to her little house and small dog, Pip. He had been cared for by a neighbour, but would be waiting for her.

Sophia loved her cottage and had taken pride and pleasure

in making it pretty. Round every corner pictures and unusual ornaments stood by in greeting. Nothing of value, just things that made her smile.

She received a rapturous welcome from Pip who, after excited squeaks and wagging of the tail, trotted after her to the kitchen. Following the suggestion of the kind police officer, she made a comforting cup of tea.

Her children would be expecting calls. In spite of aching with weariness, she got through to her daughter's number. Maisy, her granddaughter answered. 'Mum's out at a school meeting.'

'Alright, darling, I'll ring tomorrow. See you very soon.'

Her son's answering machine was on, but much as she loved them, it was a relief to be able to wait until the next day. The evening seemed long and empty. Even Pip had caught her mood, lying at her feet with a soulful look. Ready to go to bed and escape from her sadness in sleep, Sophia remembered some post. A bill, the parish magazine and a hand written envelope—a letter from Angela.

> Dear Godmother,
>
> Sorry for not being in touch for so long. You'll never guess what—Daniel has just given me your address. I've been helping him while his usual carer was away.
>
> I feel bad about not answering your letters, but to be honest, I was angry with you for a long time. When I was young you seemed to be hanging around watching my every move. I didn't know what world I was suppose to fit into and felt lost and depressed. But then I met Peter, who was amazing and helped me to understand and forgive you. I'm glad to say he is now my husband!
>
> There's so much to catch up on. Can I come and see you very soon?
>
> News in brief: I've been a carer for a while, but really good to have the nursing experience.

Dad died two years ago. His motor bike skidded into a tree. Just the way he would have wanted to go.

Mum seems fine and still enjoys going down the pub with her friends. Please write.

Lots of love,

Angela

How could she have been so naive to imagine Angela's life would be perfect, but little point in dwelling on her quite unintentional mistakes.

Waking with a start during the night, a letter to Henry must take priority.

The following morning Sophia sat with pen and paper and her usual mug of tea. It was a difficult letter to write and she pondered on how to word it for some time. Having said how sorry she was for behaving so foolishly, rather than suggesting Henry might not wish to see her again, she offered help and support in any way needed.

The letter to Angela was easy. After a long silence, Sophia couldn't wait to see her daughter again.

A brisk walk to the post box with Pip trotting at her side put Sophia in better spirits, and once home a call to Caroline would further improve them.

A male voice announced that she was through to the Harries family and one of them would ring back. Sophia was not disappointed but relieved; her story was beginning to sound pathetic to her, and Caroline didn't suffer fools. An hour later they spoke, exchanging news and gossip as old friends do.

By the evening Sophia was feeling stronger, but went to her bedroom earlier than usual. The previous night, in her anguish, she had put the log cabin out of sight on top of a cupboard. Now she sat with it on her knee and inhaled the smell of wood. It transported her back to Wales and Henry. Sometimes even without physical contact, the tenderness between them was so strong, she could almost reach out and touch it.

Tears ran down her face as she again offered up a prayer of hope that Henry would respond to her note.

Lying in bed, a full moon made the log cabin visible on a nearby table. A sudden light breeze blew the tiny door open and the cabin filled with light. A cloud then darkened the room, Sophia smiled and closed her eyes.

After some sound hours of sleep, Sophia woke next morning with renewed vigour, which propelled her out of bed earlier than usual. At the sound of her footsteps, Pip was already waiting expectantly by the door.

'Alright, little dog. I'll have a mug of tea and then we'll go out for a lovely walk.'

This news was received with obvious enthusiasm.

It was just light when they set off, and the rest of the world appeared to be still sleeping. Not a soul to be seen.

A narrow path wound through a copse, leading to open fields and orchards. Sophia never failed to appreciate being able to walk in these beautiful surroundings.

Quite suddenly, the silence was broken by an unmistakable sound. Soon it was directly above them and Sophia looked up to see a red helicopter, and knew at once that, inside that machine, were people dedicated in mind, body and spirit to caring for those in need of help. She herself had never used their services, but as it disappeared from view, she nevertheless had a great sense of pride and gratitude.

Before returning home from a walk, Sophia would often sit on a log on the path leading out of the small wood. Here she would think about the day ahead. It might be cooking for the Cool Catering Company, sitting with a hospital patient or simply enjoying friends.

Henry did not feature in these plans as regularly as she would have liked. Had she known before about the problem in his life, a great deal of pain and anxiety could have been avoided, but now she seemed better able to let go of worries, like watching a leaf float downstream and out of sight.

Today her thoughts went far back in time. She was a sixteen-year-old girl at home with her parents. At the same time a feeling that all would be well enveloped her as she remembered saying to them with absolute certainty, 'Mum and Pop, you need never worry about me, 'cos I'll always be alright,'

Sophia rose to her feet.

'Come on, Pip, let's go home.'

Sophia varied her walks each day, but did not now venture very far, as her left leg had become noticeably weaker than the other. Back at home, she would do a few stretches, learned in Imogen's small, friendly class, before carrying on with her day.

Now part of Sophia's walk routine was sternly telling herself not to be upset by hearing nothing from Henry. Today, approaching the front door, Pip gave a little bark and Sophia's stomach lurched—a Landrover. Of course he had come in person to say he no longer needed her in his life. She braced herself for what was to come.

Without even saying good morning or hello, he asked, 'Could you make me a very strong cup of coffee?' he looked miserable.

'Of course, come in.'

'I haven't been in touch—'

'I know why you're here, Henry, I'm so—'

'My sweet girl, what you said the other day was not you, so please just forget it.'

Topping up their cups, Sophia was so relieved she felt instantly reborn.

'A few days ago,' he continued, 'Joanna asked to see me on an urgent matter. Not knowing what to expect, I went there ready to help, only to be told she never wanted to see me again as she had a new man in her life who is everything I'm not. We no longer have a marriage, but I feel useless and a complete failure. May I please take up your offer of support?'

Sophia cupped his face in her hands.

'Of course you can.'

Henry seldom saw his son, who had lived abroad for most of his adult life, so getting a letter to say he would be coming to stay in a week's time, Henry was delighted and immediately enlisted Sophia to help with preparations.

When Chris finally arrived, he was a little taken aback as he had Amy, his partner whom Henry knew little about, with him and a vast amount of luggage.

Hearing Henry's voice on the telephone three days later, Sophia expected a report on their wonderful reunion. Instead he sounded upset.

'They've completely taken over my house, that is Chris and Amy, who I've never even met and they intend to stay as long as it suits, perhaps indefinitely. They're noisy and untidy—I can't stand it.'

'Henry, pack a bag and come here and make sure they pay rent.'

'It's an offer I couldn't possibly refuse and I'll be with you in time for supper, if that's alright.'

'That'll be lovely.'

Sophia sympathised with Henry's disappointment over his son's behaviour, but couldn't help being encouraged by this turn of events.

With a delicious meal ready and candles lit, he would arrive in a few minutes.

Life was about to change.

What a joy to have someone so charming and considerate under her roof. Sophia loved Henry's humour and endless stories and limericks, 'There was an old man of . . .' Sitting together in the evening, encouraged by Sophia, he talked about his marriage, his guilt and other concerns.

He received a very courteous letter one morning from Gerard, Joanna's new man, explaining that living near the home, he was happy to be called upon should Joanna need anything at any time. He was also delighted by their shared love of music. Henry very much appreciated hearing from him and wrote back immediately. Sophia observed that a previously strained look on his face had disappeared.

'I feel like a new man,' he said, giving her a bear-like hug.

Every week he would go back home to collect things and see his son. They were now on good terms; Henry had made sure of that. On these occasions, Sophia would feel a little fearful that he might not return as, after all, there was no commitment to do so. Apart from increasingly short periods of doubt, Sophia could not remember having enjoyed life so much.

Her family enthusiastically gave Henry the thumbs up and they all got together whenever possible. Cordelia with her husband and daughter, and Tancred, unmarried but always with a girl on his arm.

Sophia especially enjoyed seeing Angela, who appeared when work permitted.

Always forthright with her questions, one afternoon Angela asked, 'Fancy you having a fling with a mechanic—bit of a wild child weren't you? Maybe you were rebelling against your background?'

'There might of been an element of that,' smiled Sophia.

When they talked, she felt it important to make the point

of how much Angela was loved and wanted, never of her doubts and fears over the birth.

As the bond between she and Henry grew ever stronger, Sophia shed her insecurities, so much so that after one of their occasional disagreements she would say, 'We're not married, so feel free to leave.'

To which Henry responded, 'Well, I think I'll just stay for lunch!' neatly defusing the situation.

For about ten years they enjoyed a near-perfect life.

Sophia was always aware of the considerable age gap between herself and Henry, but now there were signs that all was not well. Although upright and trim and always taken for a younger man, Sophia noticed he was disinclined to walk any distance. She herself could no longer manage a long ramble and so they were well matched. The faithful Pip understood and adapted to shorter walkies.

With little consideration for her own health, Sophia put her fatigue to one side to help Henry. He had started coughing a lot and choking on his food, which upset and alarmed her. An appointment with a specialist proved unsatisfactory and he was unforthcoming about what was said.

Over the weeks, Henry became increasingly quiet and his appetite was very poor. One morning Sophia prepared a lovely soft-boiled egg, later finding it untouched in the bin. The local surgery then supplied food supplements which he disliked.

Sophia felt helpless and distressed as she watched Henry fade away before her eyes with obvious throat cancer. She knew any treatment suggested would be refused.

One afternoon, Sophia needed to be out for an hour. She

returned to find him in a very distressed state, so contacting the surgery an evening visit was arranged.

A pretty young female doctor appeared, perking him up considerably, but as she left Sophia had a quiet word and it was decided Henry would need to go into hospital soon. Next morning, not wanting to get up, Sophia knew the moment had come and arranged for an ambulance to collect him. It was sad to see him go, but they both knew it was the right thing.

Purely by chance, a friend was coming to stay, arriving later that morning. Elizabeth immediately understood the situation and insisted, not only on taking Sophia out for lunch, but to then drive them to the hospital.

As always, Henry rose to the occasion and was delighted to see Elizabeth, and was pleased she could visit him again with Sophia the following day.

He seemed in good heart the next afternoon and again enjoyed Elizabeth's company. She and Sophia noticed that as a polite and undemanding person, he was already liked and respected by the staff.

Elizabeth had to go home later that day and Sophia found the cottage very quiet. Having a list of people to ring about Henry helped to prevent her from feeling too isolated.

When she rang the local volunteer group, Sophia was much relieved to discover that a driver could take and return her from the hospital, thus avoiding the parking ordeal.

At the end of the week, when walking into the ward, the senior nurse took Sophia to one side.

'He's got a lot to say to you, so take as long as you like.'

Explaining the difficulty of hearing Henry through the oxygen mask, the nurse agreed it could be removed.

'But not for too long,' she advised, giving Sophia a pat on the shoulder.

They then had a wonderful talk in which everything that

needed to be said was said. After a moment's silence, Henry made an announcement, 'I've decided to leave.'

'Do you mean leave the hospital?' asked Sophia

'No, leave the Earth.'

There was nothing she could say. The option of moving to a nearby hospice had been discussed the previous day and Henry liked the idea. Sophia was already visualising peaceful times together, although probably not for long. She needed to focus on this plan.

Knowing that Pip would be left on his own for far longer than usual, Henry had told Sophia not to worry as he had ordered and paid for a taxi home.

Checking at reception on the way out, she learned that there was no taxi, the idea had been entirely in his head. Such thoughtfulness from a seriously ill man was profoundly humbling.

At 7.30 am the next morning, the telephone rang. It was the hospital to say Henry had died an hour ago. Sophia slumped into the nearest armchair, completely stunned. In seconds Pip was with her, pressing himself firmly against her leg. He knew.

The days that followed went by in a haze of activity. People rallied round, helping with formalities and in any way they could while Sophia and both families planned the cremation service.

Reflecting on the occasion made Sophia very proud of Henry as so many family and friends squeezed into her home afterwards.

To ensure every one found the cottage, Sophia had put a Moroccan lantern by the gate. Inside were four quite small candles, which despite their size, burnt brightly until late afternoon—a symbol of Henry's strong and enduring spirit.

Answering letters about his death proved great therapy and telephone calls were much appreciated. Once all of the correspondence was done and with less needing attention, the days seemed long and bleak.

A minor fracture of the pelvis turned out, for Sophia, to be a
bonus. Unable to take Pip out, a neighbour's help was enlisted.
Pip already knew Hermione, and the pair went out happily each
morning. This routine allowed Sophia and Hermione to get to
know each other well and the two became close friends.

Life was starting to become a little rosier and she made a
great effort to look outward, but one day, without warning, Pip
stopped eating, although he drank a great deal. Sophia offered
him every kind of food, but to no avail. He seemed quite lively,
but with no improvement otherwise, an appointment was made
at the surgery.

When told that Pip had cancer of the kidneys, Sophia again
went in to a state of shock. Treatment to prolong his life was
suggested but, leaving him at the surgery, she returned home
unconvinced. Going straight to the telephone she rang her very
old friend Tim, a veterinary surgeon, whose advice she valued
highly. He explained that what was proposed for Pip would keep
him going only for a limited time, often with unpleasant side-
effects. The best course of action was for him to be put to sleep.

Returning to the surgery, she said goodbye to Pip in
the waiting room; Hermione had accompanied her, having
volunteered to be there while he peacefully slipped away. Sophia
could not face being with him, so she waited in the car feeling
completely devastated.

The cottage was desolate without Pip, and was made worse
by the presence of his bed, lead and toys, so Sophia gathered
them up and put them out of sight in a shed, ready to go to
charity. Beautiful photographs of him, taken by Henry, were all
she needed.

At bedtime, Sophia thought tearfully of their nightly routine
when, kneeling by Pip's bed, he would put a paw on her hand.

Just before becoming ill, one night, he gently touched her face and she felt the roughness of his pads on her cheek. Was he saying goodbye?

For many years Sophia had lived with numbness and tingling hands and feet. Seeking advice from a number of professionals, none had an answer, so she simply lived with it. But now, in addition to walking becoming more difficult, loss of balance was also a cause for concern and she went to see her GP.

Describing her symptoms to a very nice female doctor, the response was to arrange an MRI scan.

On the day of the appointment, Sophia arrived at the hospital with little idea of what to expect. It was not a pleasant experience, but by imaging herself on an exotic tropical island, she got through it without pressing the 'get me out of here' button.

With the results back from the hospital, Sophia returned to the doctor.

'It's MS,' she said very quietly, 'but many of my patients lead a normal life.'

This was good news. Sophia had heard of the condition, but had no knowledge of how it might progress.

When he was alive, Henry would willingly buy and carry their shopping home. Now unable to do this, a workable plan for Sophia was driving to the next village where the post office and store had parking a few steps from the door. Run by a helpful family, one of them could carry groceries to the car for her. The often heard 'must be near the shops' was, for her, no use at all.

In a mildly irritating way, when asked, 'Are you still driving?' she felt that she was actually being presented with a challenge.

One day Sophia's answer was, 'Yes, and I'm planning to go to Scotland in my little jeep.'

Realising this to be a little over ambitious, the distance was reduced and she plumped for Cumbria.

With arrangements made and bags packed, Sophia set off for Lincoln to stay with a cousin. Despite a long, hot drive, she was ready to move on after two enjoyable days.

A north-westerly route took her on quiet roads through lovely countryside and eventually to her destination and a welcome from another cousin.

Without knowing beforehand, the visit was perfectly timed as each day when she and Emma went out for a picnic or pub lunch, lines of Romany wagons, freshly painted and decorated, could be seen making their way to Appleby Fair. This spectacle was a treat for Sophia having had, since childhood, an interest and affinity with the gypsy way of life.

When another lovely visit was over, Sophia went a different way south, staying en route with family. Safely home, she enjoyed a sense of achievement, though realistically knowing it would be the last 'grand tour.'

Next morning, the MS nurse called at the cottage. Sophia liked Ginny immediately. A rare being who, despite a huge number of patients, somehow managed to see them all. If questions came up she could be contacted in her office and would always return calls.

When the front gate needed repairs, a useful contact was made through Hermione who knew just the person for the job. She appeared one afternoon with Sebastian 'call me Seb.' He and Sophia made a date and work was soon underway.

During their elevenses one day, the gate mended but in need of a coat of paint, Sophia mentioned a well-known TV chef who cooked in what appeared to be a garden shed. Could Seb transform her kitchen into something similar? Some handymen might consider a request like this rather odd, but not Seb, who was immediately enthusiastic. Creative ideas then bounced back and forth between them like ping pong balls. This was not to be a built-in, planned kitchen, so it evolved as work progressed, taking on its own identity. Shelves were not straight planks of wood, but curved, with circles, diamond shapes and oblongs at either end.

Having a niece with MS, Seb knew about high dosage oxygen therapy and offered to take Sophia to the centre.

Finding it friendly and helpful, she booked in for a session. However, after a few times experiencing great discomfort in the ears, coupled with a long, tiring drive home, Sophia decided not to go again. Had there been a convenient husband or partner to drive her, continuing might have been a possibility.

Progression of the MS continued almost in slow motion, allowing Sophia to adapt when necessary. Her steep stairs was sometimes manageable, but often not. The layout was unsuitable for a stair lift, so she decided to sleep downstairs permanently.

Still keen to maintain independence, when in need of a cup of tea or tasty meal, Sophia preferred to get it herself, though had a delicious little something occasionally appeared magically on a tray . . . lovely!

Sophia managed in a way that worked for her, needing help only once a week with shopping and cleaning. She still enjoyed cooking, and preparation could be done sitting at the kitchen table, though standing over the pots and pans was becoming difficult. To move around the house, Sophia had a three-wheeler 'thingy' as she called it, but admitting to vanity, avoided being seen using it, preferring two sticks when visitors came, or for going out. Her aim was to stay on her feet for as long as possible.

Getting to and from the car on a short path was manageable, but longer drives were now tiring. The problem was solved by obtaining the appropriate railcard which proved a helpful service. It was many years since she had used a train and she enjoyed looking out at the beautiful scenery, but was saddened to observe that most passengers appeared to be permanently looking at some sort of screen.

Seb continued to come up with useful ideas. Knowing Sophia was adamant the house should not look like a nursing home, instead of grab rails, he put up pretty brass handles. He also encouraged her to keep going with her craft work. The production line included collage, card making, cork boards and mosaics.

There seemed little point in planning for the future, MS being a condition making it difficult to do so. Therefore Sophia lived day-by-day and life was as good as it could be. But something appalling was about to happen.

On a bright summer morning, Sophia left the house expecting to return by late afternoon. She didn't—and would not see her cottage for about three months.

From mid-afternoon that day, Sophia had only brief periods of being conscious. Kind voices, her clothes being cut off and looking up to see the rotating blades of a helicopter; so very noisy.

She came to lying on a bed having no idea where she was. There was no fear or pain, but someone was telling her of serious injuries suffered when, as a passenger, the car had impacted with something very solid.

Shocked and in a weakened state, Sophia was put into a single ward. As a patient in a large teaching hospital, she received the best possible care and treatment and, with little delay, an operation took place on her two broken femurs which necessitated the use of plates and screws.

If this were not enough, it soon became apparent that another internal procedure was necessary, and she was told that beforehand a blood transfusion would be given.

In the past Sophia had donated regularly and on reaching

fifty pints, she had been presented with a certificate and two mugs. Giving was the easy part; receiving quite another matter and would apparently take most of the night.

Coming safely through the operation, it was nevertheless a set back and some days, when a son or daughter sat by the bed, Sophia felt too poorly to talk and could only hold a hand.

They say things come in threes, and Sophia then developed a bladder infection. Many years ago, renal colic had been her most painful experience, and this came a very close second, leaving her unable to eat for a week.

Slowly improving in health and strength, she was able to appreciate all the uplifting messages and cards arriving daily. Living nearest, Cordelia visited most days often with her husband. Sophia was extremely grateful for her unfailing support, her skill at extracting information and getting answers to questions.

Time dragged on and Sophia was keen to be moved to her local hospital. At last, after a frustrating wait, a bed became available.

Back on home territory, she found herself in another large single ward overlooking a pleasant garden. Local friends could call in, though others nobly travelled some distance.

Sophia knew the importance of physiotherapy in aiding recovery and she had reached the stage of attempting to stand. An alarming looking frame was provided for this, which she found difficult and made her nervous. Hospital life had its cheerful moments, however, one being when a friend who lived nearby and often called in with delicious snacks, suggested that as Sophia was on no medication, a glass of wine could feature on the evening menu—great news.

After so many weeks in two hospitals, Sophia longed for home. Tancred had arranged for the ground floor of the cottage to be levelled and other necessary work to meet his mother's needs. A wonderful gesture, but one that would take time, so for the final weeks Sophia moved into a care home. Before leaving, she worked on getting in and out of bed without help, especially at night. Her persistence paid off and the goal was achieved.

The long-awaited day arrived with the cottage ready for Sophia's return. Although wonderful to be back, she was not the same person, lacking in confidence and unsure of her future capabilities. Her helpful lodger, though often away, was there the first night, but all was well.

Apart from a little daytime help, she was suddenly alone, trying to adapt to a different life, such as using a wheelchair. Although something she had fought against, it did help to conserve energy. With a number of things she was now unable to do, there were low times when Sophia told friends that 'a slice of my life has been stolen.'

Much appreciated was the kindness and encouragement shown by friends and family, but a few crossed the fine line of being very helpful to controlling. Occasionally, usually one of the older generation, thought it perfectly acceptable to comment on her mobility. Sophia would remain silent at the time knowing any response to be unrepeatable! At moments such as these, anger, she found, could be beneficial when channelled into a determination to make life better in some way.

After Henry died and Sophia had settled on the ground floor, she was able to offer a lovely spare room to lodgers. For around four years several had been and gone, all very different people, but almost without exception spontaneously helpful. In fact, the partner of one became girl Friday to Sophia. A very happy arrangement. Despite a few sceptics and having no expectations, the experience so far had been most heartening.

Since being back in the cottage, it seemed to Sophia that the MS had obligingly stepped aside, allowing her injuries to heal as much as they could and for her confidence to grow. Vital to well-being, she was grateful that her creative force was undiminished. Seb, aware of this, could be relied upon to help with cutting wood to size if needed for the next project.

Now that activities were more limited for Sophia, the company of friends was much appreciated and one afternoon, whilst putting the world to rights over a cup of tea, Imogen asked, 'Sophia, you have been through a lot over the past sixteen months, I'd love to know if there's anything you find particularly helpful?'

'What works for me may not for others. I'm drawn to certain books that inspire and mantras for an instant boost. I sense Henry's energy around me and his continuing encouragement and support, just as it was when he was on the earth. There will be those who are sceptical, but I accept that.'

'The important thing is that it helps you,' said Imogen, delighted that her friend felt able to share thoughts and ideas.

'It's good to talk—as they say—and our chats are always stimulating and interesting, a real tonic,' enthused Sophia.

'Did I tell you my dear friend Guy is arriving to stay this evening and he is going to cook?'

'Lucky you,' replied Imogen. 'And will you be starting with a cocktail?'

'I don't know,' answered Sophia, 'but as it's only a few days till Christmas, why don't we put some ingredients together?'

'I'll put in love and gratitude and add a measure of fortitude and empathy,' suggested Imogen.

'Harmony, hope and being non-judgmental can be poured in, and we mustn't forget a large measure of fun and laughter,' added Sophia.

Imogen suddenly looked at her watch, 'Goodness, look at the time. I must go home and wrap some presents.'

Sophia watched her go down the path and through the gate, but did not immediately shut the door.

Snow had fallen, silently, just a covering, creating a sparkling, beautiful scene. Nature's offering for the cocktail.

Books of Wisdom, Comfort and Courage

Letting Go by David R. Hawkins

Proof of Heaven: A Neurosurgeon's Journey into the Afterlife by Eben Alexander

Feel the Fear and Do It Anyway: How to Turn Your Fear and Indecision into Confidence and Action by Susan Jeffers

The Spy Who Loved by Clare Mulley

The Tibetan Book of Living And Dying by Sogyal Rinpoche

Mind of a Survivor: What the Wild has Taught Me about Survival and Success by Megan Hine

The Dalai Lama's Cat by David Michie

Happiness: A Guide to Developing Life's Most Important Skill by Matthieu Ricard

Acknowledgements

I should like to thank Dan of Aspect Design for his patience and help with this book. It was especially enjoyable working together on ideas for the cover and to see it evolve was very exciting.